James Philip

———————

When Winter Comes

———————

UNTIL THE NIGHT – BOOK FOUR

Copyright © James P. Coldham writing as James Philip, in respect of When Winter Comes, Book 4 of the Until the Night Series (the serialisation of the 2nd Edition of Until the Night), 2015. All rights reserved.

Cover concept by James Philip
Graphic Design by Beastleigh Web Design

The Bomber War Series

Book 1: Until the Night
Book 2: The Painter
Book 3: The Cloud Walkers

Until the Night Series

A serialisation of Book 1: Until the Night in five parts

Part 1: Main Force Country – September 1943
Part 2: The Road to Berlin – October 1943
Part 3: The Big City – November 1943
Part 4: When Winter Comes – December 1943
Part 5: After Midnight – January 1944

When Winter Comes

People talk a lot about picking out targets and bombing them, individual small targets – in the European climate? I've come to the conclusion that people who say that sort of thing not only have never been outside, but they've never looked out of a window.

Attacks on cities are strategically justified in so far as they tend to shorten the war and so preserve the lives of allied soldiers.

Air Marshall Sir Arthur Harris
[Air Officer Commanding-in-Chief RAF Bomber Command]

Chapter 1

Thursday 2nd December, 1943
RAF Ansham Wolds, Lincolnshire

For the third day in a row Bomber Command's heavies had been warned for Berlin. Both previous attacks had been cancelled late in the day and once again the weather threatened to spoil the party. However, Adam was in no mood to concede the possibility that tonight's operation might go the way of its two predecessors. That morning and throughout the early afternoon he had driven the Squadron into a frenzy of activity. Any hint of complacency, of slacking, of pausing to contemplate the likelihood of another cancellation was stamped upon and ruthlessly eradicated.

He was determined that if the attack went ahead 647 Squadron would be ready. More than ready, positively yearning for the off. Four of his Lancasters had failed flight tests, leaving twenty fit for ops. Six tons of 100-octane and four-and-a-half tons of bombs was being pumped and winched into each of these aircraft as the main crew briefing drew to an end.

"The AP lies to the east of the industrial Wittenau District. Tonight, the object of the exercise is to hit the north-western sector of Berlin. With the exception of the Siemensstadt complex, this area is the most heavily industrialised part of city. Factories in the target area produce tanks, heavy artillery, locomotives, rolling stock and all manner of other vital manufactures for the Nazi war machine."

He surveyed the faces of *his* crews, wondering how many more times he would stand before *his* Squadron. He wondered also how much longer the Squadron he had inherited from Bert Fulshawe would survive as recognisably the same Squadron; now that the Main Force was locked in battle with the Big City disaster lurked at every turn.

Herman Jablonski and Hector Angelis, the Squadron's guests for the night's entertainment, sat in the front row hemmed in by aircrew. Jablonski, the larger, and more florid of the pair scribbled noisily in the hush. He was jotting down Adam's every word. His companion, Hector Angelis was subdued, a little listless. Perhaps, the waiting was preying on his mind. Not so for Herman Jablonski who had become more animated and more excitable as take off approached.

Adam launched into his concluding remarks.

Crossing the Dutch coast below Alkmaar, the outward route was dead straight all the way to Berlin. On the final approach to the target, all aircraft equipped with *H2S* - including 7 of his 20 Lancasters - were to attempt to line up on the target using the radar indications of the towns of Stendal, Rathenow and Nauen. Over the target the Pathfinders would employ the now standard Berlin Method; with blind markers and backer-up aircraft releasing every kind of TI and Sky Marker at their disposal regardless of the visibility, throughout the attack. The attack was timed to commence at 20:04 and to last 20 minutes.

It would be the fifth attack on the German capital in a fortnight.

Adam sensed the grim resolution of his crews. They were committed to the long haul against Berlin and it was likely to be the death of most of them. He was proud, humbled.

"Right, chaps," he drawled, picking up his trusty billiard cue. "I know I've said it before, but nevertheless, I shall say it again." He tapped the point of the cue on the big, dirty smudge which dominated the top right-hand corner of the map of north-western Europe. "The metropolitan area of Berlin in nineteen thirty-nine was reliably measured at eight hundred and eighty-three square miles. Tonight, it will take you twenty-five minutes to fly across the Berlin defended zone. If you chaps can't find a hole in the flak somewhere over the target to drop your bombs through, well, frankly, I shall be very surprised!" This provoked a low rumble of amusement. Next, he got the evening's debutants on their feet: two sprog crews opening their account with 647 Squadron. "As I say, chaps. You won't have any problem finding the target tonight. They'll be hundreds of bloody searchlights! Flak thick enough to walk home on! The main thing is to remember to drop your bombs before you get shot down!"

The old lags laughed.

Adam waited for the hall to quieten.

"A final word. The last two ops were scrubbed late in the day. Today's show will go ahead. Take it from me, today's show will go ahead. I won't have anybody going through the motions, or getting careless. I won't have it! When you get out to your kites re-check everything before the off as if your lives depend on it. Your lives do depend on it!

Don't relax! Don't get sloppy!"

The latest forecast predicted the afternoon mist over the Yorkshire airfields would worsen, grounding 4 and 6 Group's Halifaxes, and reducing the Main Force's overall strength by over a hundred heavies. Tonight, there was unlikely to be a shield of lower-flying Halifaxes betwixt the fighters and his Lancasters over Germany.

"Good luck, gentlemen."

Herman Jablonski pursued Adam outside, caught up with him as he sauntered over to the Operations Room.

"Quite a speech, Wing-Commander."

Adam shrugged. "One does one's best."

He was uncomfortably aware that the newsman, not content with being offered a ring-side seat over Berlin, was hot on the trail of a 'personal' angle on the story. He was looking for a hero, or failing that, a villain. Adam did not care to be either. Recognition, and a degree of celebrity amongst one's fellows was one thing, a broader fame and a niche in the public eye was another. However much pleasure he derived, secretly or otherwise from the former, he had no appetite whatsoever for the latter. Guy Gibson was welcome to his place in the spotlight, lonely in the hideous glare of public adulation. Little good had it done him.

"So, how many missions have you flown?"

"Sixty, seventy, something like that," Adam replied, fending off the interrogation as best he could. "A lot of them were milk runs, of course."

"Like that raid on the Graf Zeppelin?"

"Well, er, no. That wasn't exactly a milk run," he conceded. How on earth did the blasted man know about the Gdynia raid last year?

Herman Jablonski pounced. "Nine hundred miles from base. Bombing an aircraft carrier in a heavily defended port at low-level. That's one Helluva milk run, Wing-Commander!"

"We didn't actually bomb the Graf Zeppelin," Adam reminded him. "It was a bit foggy. We couldn't find the bloody thing. We ended up bombing the docks."

"No, no, no! It's no use being modest. The people back home want to hear about guys like you. Believe me."

"Oh, I doubt it, Mister Jablonski."

"Herman," demanded the American. "Herman!"

"The thing is," Adam went on. "Er, Herman. I'm just a chap doing a job, that's all."

"What is it with you guys?" Exclaimed the American, exasperated. "What are you afraid of? What's the problem?"

Adam stopped suddenly. Jablonski skidded past him, turned to face him. The other man was in his thirties, overweight, out of breath from hurrying to snare his victim. He breathed heavily, momentarily lost for words.

"Herman, I don't want to be rude…"

"But?" Grinned the American.

"I'll answer your questions about the Squadron, tonight's op and matters arising. However, as for what 'the people back home' want to hear about 'guys like me', well, that's too bad. So far as I'm concerned that's not part of the contract. You are here to fly an op to Berlin and that's exactly what you will do. Write what you want but please, leave me out of it."

Herman Jablonski was hugely amused by his naivety. Amused but not surprised. Three days hanging around kicking his heels waiting for the weather to clear had given him ample time to sample the atmosphere of Ansham Wolds, and to measure of the temper of its people. In October he had visited an 8th Air Force field in Suffolk in the aftermath of the second disastrous Schweinfurt mission. Sixty Fortresses had fallen that day, over twenty percent of the entire American heavy bomber force. Since then the Fighting Eighth had been licking its wounds. However, had he been pumping the commander of a B-17 Squadron the talk would have been of missions, objectives, and mean circular bombing error. The Fighting Eighth was driven by its 'mission', its sacred duty to prove that the pin-point bombing of key industrial and military targets by day would win the war, but as yet the Fortresses had flown nowhere near Berlin. Unlike the boys in the Fortresses, the kids in Chantrey's Lancasters literally had their hands around the enemy's throat. Every time they flew to Germany they were tightening the noose around the enemy's neck. Nobody at Ansham Wolds had any doubt that they were 'making a difference', or that they were 'doing their bit', you could see it in their faces and in the way they held themselves. Nobody bothered to talk about morale or *esprit de corps* here in Lincolnshire. They had no need to talk about it: it was all around them, in the air, a tangible, almost touchable thing. And in the middle of it all was an enigma, the man people in the Mess at Bawtry had called 'the low-level king', Adam Chantrey.

"Sorry, pal," Jablonski laughed. "It doesn't work that way." And it never had. The more the younger man clammed up the more curious he became. "Look, I'm on your side. I'm here to put you guys' side of the story."

"I didn't realise we had a side?" Adam countered. "I thought we were all supposed to be on the same side?"

"You know what I mean."

"I'm afraid I don't. And unfortunately, I don't have time to discuss it further. If you'll excuse me, I shall get on."

Even Herman Jablonski realised that for the moment, at least, he had come to the end of the line.

"See you later, Wing-Commander," he waved.

Chapter 2

Thursday 2nd December, 1943
RAF Ansham Wolds, Lincolnshire

A premature, wintery dusk was falling across the airfield as the first Merlins coughed, flamed, and bellowed into life. Herman Jablonski, the son of a Silesian émigré, was returning to the homeland of his parents aboard a British bomber bound for Berlin. He had asked the famous Wing-Commander if there was anything he wanted to say before they took off.

"For the record?"

"No, nothing for 'the record'. Just be a good fellow and keep out of the way, Herman," Adam Chantrey had replied, smiling.

O-Orange's broken-nosed rear gunner had eyed Jablonski malevolently all the way out to the aircraft. "Don't worry about Taffy," Ben Hardiman, the bomber's battle-scarred, towering navigator had chuckled reassuringly as they bounced and jolted in the back of the Bedford lorry. "He doesn't like anybody. Germans, Italians, French, Yanks, English. Especially the English. He's very fair-minded, that way."

"Right." Jablonski liked the navigation leader. There was none of the stiffness, nor any of the cold politeness of his pilot in Ben. Hardiman was an up-front kind of guy. You knew exactly where you were with his sort.

"We'd get rid of the little beggar," Ben had explained loudly, gesturing at the diminutive

Welshman, who snorted in defiance. "But he's the best gunner on the Squadron and the smug little bugger knows it. Don't you, Taffy!"

The gunner muttered something under his breath. Jablonski could have sworn that he said: "Fucking officers!" But everybody, Chantrey included, had laughed heartily and the W/T operator, a sallow, sharp-eyed man who was older than the others, had slapped Taffy on the back with such force he nearly bowled the smaller man over.

Before anybody boarded the aircraft, Chantrey and the flight engineer, a pale, stiff man with a precise, clipped way of speaking to the American's ear, inspected the Lancaster, minutely scrutinising control surfaces, searching for anything out of place. Only when both men were satisfied, did the pilot call to the rest of the crew.

"Okay, chaps. Mount up." As Jablonski stood behind the pilot's seat witnessing the preliminaries, his excitement slowly gave way to a nagging anxiety. Around him the crew made themselves at home and the banter circulated, everything seemed perfectly relaxed, controlled, routine. Except for the fact that none of this was routine, and none of this was in any way normal.

Suddenly, or so it seemed, Adam Chantrey decided it was time to go to work and the mood changed in a moment. "Let's get on with it, Ted," he declared, turning to the engineer.

"Roger, Skipper!" Acknowledged the other man.
"Switches off...SWITCHES OFF!"
"Inner tanks on...INNER TANKS ON!"
"Immersed pumps on...IMMERSED PUMPS ARE ON, SKIPPER!"

Jablonski guessed both men could do the drill in their sleep.

"Check seat secure!" Ted Hallowes prompted, raising his voice against the rising crescendo of Merlins firing up in the murk around them at nearby dispersals. "CHECKED SECURE."

"Brakes on and pressure up...BRAKES ON AND PRESSURE IS OK!"

"Undercarriage locked...LOCKED!"

Chantrey began to call down the engine controls checks. Hallowes fell into step, following his lead.

"Master engine cocks...OFF. Throttles...HALF-INCH OPEN. Prop controls ...FULLY UP. Slow-running cut-out switches...SET TO IDLE CUT-OFF. Supercharger controls...M RATIO. Warning light...NO WARNING LIGHT SHOWING. Air intake heat control...READS COLD. Radiator shutters...RAD SHUTTER OVER-RIDE SWITCHES ARE SET TO AUTOMATIC, SKIPPER."

Chantrey shifted in his seat, scanned the dials before him. He sighed, and briefly clenched his gloved fists.

"Right, Ted. Prepare to start up."

"Okay. We're ready to start up, Skipper!"

"Tank selector cock...TURNED TO NUMBER TWO TANK. Master engine cock on...ON. Booster pump...ON."

Chantrey slid back the cockpit window and made a thumbs up signal to the crew manning the battery cart. Jablonski glimpsed an arm raised in acknowledgment.

"Contact port-inner!" Shouted the pilot, flicking the cover off the starter button, jamming it hard into its socket. Instantly, grey-blue smoke shot through with a spurt of crimson flame belched from the exhausts of the Merlin. The engine turned once, twice then faster than a man could count. The whole aircraft shook. The Merlin ran true, awesomely, magnificently true. O-Orange hummed with the power of that one engine, its frame reverberating softly.

It was the thunder of the Merlin that finally convinced Jablonski that he was really going to war. Up until then the whole thing had seemed a little surreal, dreamlike. Now the point of no return rushed towards him. He swallowed, his mouth suddenly dry. Bone dry.

"Slow-running cut-out control!"

"SET TO ENGINE-RUNNING POSITION!" Hallowes yelled above the smooth, murderous roar of the port-inner Merlin.

Within minutes all four of O-Orange's engines were firing and Chantrey disengaged the booster coil switch, liberating the aircraft from the ground. The thunder of the Merlins shut out the world. Jablonski watched the pilot turn the ground/flight switch to FLIGHT and wave away the ground crew. He saw the erks wheeling the battery cart clear of the Lancaster.

"DR Compass...ON AND SET, SKIPPER!"

"Rad shutters...OVER-RIDE SWITCHES SET AT OPEN!"

Finally, there were the magneto tests. Presently, Adam craned his neck, looked up at Jablonski. "Everything's working, Herman," he reported. "If you've got any second thoughts, speak now or forever hold your peace."

Jablonski grinned.

"Second thoughts! You must be kidding! I wouldn't miss this for the world, Skipper!"

Adam met his eye and smiled a wan smile. The two men exchanged a nod of mutual respect. Then it was back to business.

"Pilot to bomb-aimer. Wake up, Angus!" Adam called over the intercom.

Hallowes tapped Jablonski's arm, plugged in his intercom. "Remember to unplug yourself if you leave the cockpit!" He shouted.

"Understood!"

Jablonski heard the crew members reporting in. The intercom crackled and hissed.

"Are you hearing all this, Herman?" Adam inquired when he had spoken to everybody else. "If so, hold your oxygen mask to your face and flick the switch."

Jablonski did as he was told. "I'm hearing you, Skipper!"

"Good man. The form is that you don't speak unless you're spoken to, Herman. Savvy?"

"Understood, Skipper." Ben Hardiman had briefed him about the use of the intercom when they were in the flight room waiting to be taken out to the aircraft.

"The Wingco won't have chit chat over the intercom. The intercom's for business only. Now and then you'll hear the Wingco chivvying the chaps along a bit, but otherwise we keep the channel free."

"Oh. No exceptions, then?"

"Well, if you see a fighter I think the Wingco would probably like to know about it," chortled the navigation leader. "But otherwise, no exceptions."

Jablonski listened.

"Engineer to pilot," Ted Hallowes reported over the intercom. "Hatches closed and secure. Okay to taxi, Skipper!"

Chantrey leaned out of the cockpit window and gestured for the ground crew to haul away the chocks. Jablonski saw erks disappear below the churning arc of the port-inner Merlin's propeller, saw them emerge dragging the big, heavy wooden chocks. The pilot shut the window. With a hiss of escaping air he released the brakes and the bomber jolted out onto the perimeter road. Although other Lancasters were starting up all around the field they had the road to themselves, pride of place. Tonight, O-Orange was leader of the pack. Jablonski thought this was a nice touch, wondered briefly if it was for his benefit. He suspected not. Chantrey and his crew were consummate professionals, hardly likely to alter the normal drill just for his benefit. No, Adam Chantrey was a man who led from the front and that was exactly what he was doing tonight.

The inner Merlins idled as Chantrey manoeuvred the Lancaster by juggling the outer throttles, gunning first left and then right. Jablonski turned around, looked back down the perimeter road. One by one the rest of 647 Squadron's Lancasters joined the lengthening queue behind O-Orange's tail.

The Lancaster lined-up for takeoff, halted at the threshold. "Auto-controls - clutch...IN. Cock...OUT. D.R. Compass...NORMAL. Pitot head heater switch...ON. Trimming tabs...ELEVATOR SLIGHTLY FORWARD - RUDDER NEUTRAL -

AILERON IS NEUTRAL. Prop controls...FULLY UP. Fuel...MASTER ENGINE COCKS ARE ON - TANK SELECTOR COCKS SET TO NUMBER TWO TANKS - CROSS FEED COCK IS OFF - BOOSTER PUMPS IN NUMBERS ONE AND TWO TANKS ARE ON. Superchargers...MOD. Air intake...COLD. Rad shutter switches...AUTOMATIC. Flaps...FIFTEEN DEGREES DOWN."

Jablonski saw Chantrey slide his right hand into position behind the throttles, ease the levers forward up to zero boost against the brakes. The response was even, he throttled back. The runway stretched away into the distance, its far end shrouded in the dusk.

"Clear to take-off, Skipper!" Hallowes shouted. Then he leaned over his pilot's shoulder and placed his hand behind Chantrey's on the throttles.

"Lock throttles...LOCKED!"

Adam flicked on his intercom with his left hand. "Pilot to crew. Prepare for take-off." One last deep breath, then: "Pilot to rear-gunner. Okay behind?"

"Rear gunner to Skipper. OKAY BEHIND!"

Adam pressed the throttles forward. When he reached zero boost he released the brakes. O-Orange picked up speed. Opening the throttles he advanced those for the port Merlins slightly ahead of those for the starboard pair, countering the torque. Over-burdened, weighed down, the bomber shuddered and strained as she accelerated down the runway. A touch on the brakes and her tail lifted off the wet tarmac. Jablonski caught a glimpse of the droves of cheering well-wishers at the side of the runway, in a trance he waved back at the crowd. Hallowes was shouting the increasing speeds as Chantrey held the charging bomber arrow-straight along the centreline of the runway.

"Seventy...Seventy-five..."

"Full power!" Chantrey demanded, taking his hand off the throttles.

"Full power!" Hallowes repeated, pushing the throttles hard up against their stops. "Eighty...Eight-five...Ninety...Ninety-five...One hundred...And five...Ten..."

Still Chantrey held the bomber down. Jablonski caught sight of the end of the runway, saw the tall, barbed wire topped fence in the distance, coming closer, rushing closer.

"One hundred and fifteen...twenty..."

Hallowes never once looked out of the cockpit. Jablonski contemplated shutting his eyes, forced himself to look at the runway's end racing toward him. The aircraft was shaking violently, rattling, whistling over the tarmac. Jablonski clung to the armoured back of the Pilot's seat, his knuckles white, his eyes wide with alarm. The warning markings at the end of the runway flashed under O-Orange's nose. The furrows in the field beyond the perimeter fence were plainly visible.

Then Chantrey hauled back on the controls and miraculously, most of the shaking and buffeting stopped and the Lancaster steadied.

"Climbing power! NOW!"

Hallowes pushed the throttles through the gate. O-Orange soared high over the perimeter fence.

"Wheels up."

Jablonski dared to breathe again.

"Jeeeez..." He muttered to himself.

Chapter 3

Thursday 2nd December, 1943
Lancaster O-Orange, 5 miles West of Rathenow

The intercom crackled. Up ahead ranks of searchlights groped for prey four miles high over Berlin, flak flashed on and off in a deadly umbrella. O-Orange shouldered into and through the backwash of an unseen heavy.

Behind his blackout curtain Ben viewed what he thought was the town of Rathenow sliding down the shimmering tube of his *H2S* set. Something was wrong. Very wrong. He flicked the switch on his face mask, spoke in the clipped, precise way he only spoke when there was a problem.

"Navigator to pilot. Please say again. Where are the TIs going down?"

"Pilot to navigator." Adam tensed, wanting to know what was wrong. "Red TIs and Sky Markers at three o'clock. No other major concentration of TIs in sight."

"Roger, Skipper. Recommend we hold this course, out."

Adam read volumes into this. Ben thought the Pathfinders had got it wrong. Again. However, there was no pressing operational need to share this information with the rest of the crew. Not yet.

"Hold on zero-nine-five, out."

Ben scrabbled with his charts, re-checked. The Pathfinders had got the winds wrong. The cross wind had blown the blind markers off track by as much as twenty miles to the south. Unaware of the mis-forecast winds, the openers had inadvertently lined up on the towns of Genthin, Brandenburg and Potsdam. These towns would have presented *H2S* signatures similar, if not identical to Stendal, Rathenow and Nauen. Consequently, the Pathfinders were dropping their markers over the south-western suburbs of the city, possibly to the south of the Zehlendorf or Lichterfelde Districts. The Main Force, flying on the coat tails of the openers was about to start bombing open countryside. Mile upon mile of virtually uninhabited, open countryside.

"Mid-upper gunner to pilot. Fighter flares at two o'clock, range ten miles!"

Herman Jablonski listened to the reports flowing over the intercom. The gunners had reported combats at regular intervals all the way from the Dutch coast but little had happened in O-Orange's immediate vicinity.

This changed in a moment.

"Rear-Gunner to pilot. Combat astern at ten o'clock. Range two miles. Heavy going down on fire."

"Navigator to pilot," Ben called, tersely. "I believe the Pathfinders are marking an area at least fifteen, possibly as many as twenty miles to the south of the planned AP. Repeat. The markers are going down at least fifteen miles due south of the correct position."

"Roger, navigator," Adam acknowledged without further comment. If Ben said the Pathfinders had got it wrong that was good enough for him. Further discussion was superfluous. "In that case we will hold this course and do a timed bombing run from the next available datum point," he decided, without ado. "Nauen, I assume?"

"Nauen, Skipper," Ben confirmed. "I'm working on it now, over."

O-Orange droned on towards the inferno. A handful of blind markers seemed to have realised, belatedly, that the main pattern was wide of the mark. Scattered TIs and Sky Markers were falling north of the original concentration, albeit still several miles off target.

"Looks like we've got five-tenths cloud over the target, chaps," Adam announced, casually, almost idly.

"Rear gunner to pilot. A Lanc just exploded. Astern, about one mile. Didn't see a fighter."

Herman Jablonski craned his neck to see ahead. Black specks crawled through the dazzle of the searchlights, Lancasters crabbing slowly across the city. In the south brilliant Sky Markers drifted on the wind. On the ground splashes of iridescent red and green marked the impacts of target indicators. Lines of flares trailed from west to east, fighter flares dropped to guide the hunters to their victims. A plume of flame to port marked the fall of another heavy. Bob Marshall in the mid-upper turret reported, matter of factly, an exploding Lancaster on the starboard beam.

Jablonski could not understand how O-Orange's crew could be so matter of fact, detached. Nor how the pilot could hold the bomber so straight and level above the breaking waves of flak while all about them searchlights weaved.

"Herman," Chantrey called, his tone conversational. "The blue-tinged searchlights are radar-controlled masters. They are linked to heavy-calibre flak batteries. The white jobs are slaves. Parts of the bomber stream must be fairly condensed because it looks like *Window* is snowing the fire control radars, you can tell this because the slaves seem to be waving about all over the shop tonight."

Jablonski absorbed this without daring to reply. The pilot might have been describing the scenery as they took a leisurely drive through the Lincolnshire countryside on a balmy summer afternoon. Eventually, after what seemed like an age, O-Orange's bomb load tumbled into a darkened patch of the city.

The Lancaster reared up and Adam advanced the throttles, pushed the nose down into a shallow dive. Normally, he would have held O-Orange rigidly on course until Round Again reported the photoflash flare had gone off. Tonight, in the corner of his eye, at the very edge of his peripheral vision he thought he saw something moving. Bracing himself, he let the Lancaster drift to starboard, rolled the aircraft ten degrees to port.

"Pilot to mid-upper gunner," he rasped into the intercom. "Search port, NOW!"

"Roger, Skipper!"

The back of Adam's neck tingled and involuntarily he glanced over his left shoulder.

What had he seen?

"Fighter at twelve o'clock level. He hasn't seen us yet, Skipper!"

Adam risked another look. He had not seen the fighter. What he had seen was another Lancaster flying above but parallel to O-Orange, about three hundred yards away. Tracer suddenly arched into, through and past the other aircraft.

"Herman," he heard himself say. "If you care to look over to your left you'll probably see a Lancaster blow up in a moment or two."

Jablonski thought he was joking.

Nevertheless, he swung around. Just to be sure. Just in case. Just in time to see the other bomber's wing tanks light up the night. There was a finger of flame, a stream of crimson against the blackness of the northern sky. Seconds later the stricken heavy blew up. A huge, blinding red and white ball of fire momentarily turning night into day.

"Jeeez…"

Chapter 4

Friday 3rd December, 1943
RAF Ansham Wolds, Lincolnshire

The Lancaster Force had had a bad night. There was no denying it. The winds that had driven the Pathfinders to the south had also caught out the majority of Main Force navigators. Countless aircraft had bombed open country south and west of the target. Then, thinking they were twenty miles further north than they actually were, many aircraft had mistakenly flown back across the whole width of the Berlin defensive zone, running the gauntlet of the flak and the searchlights a second time instead of flying away in relative safety well to the north of the city. A large number of aircraft had gone down over the Big City. Thereafter, the winds had scattered the bomber stream over a sixty mile front, stripping away its radar-baffling shield of *Window*. A number of heavies had strayed south over Hanover and Osnabruck, been coned by dozens of searchlights and systematically shot to pieces; night fighters had worked the route all the way to the Dutch coast, picking off stragglers.

Herman Jablonski looked in on Adam before he departed Ansham Wolds.

"I just came to say goodbye," he said. "And to say thanks."

Adam came around his desk and shook the big American's hand.

"It was an experience," Jablonski grimaced.

"I'm sorry about your colleague."

The other man shrugged. Mick Ferris's Z-Zebra, carrying Hector Angelis, was one of the Squadron's two lost sheep. The other was C-Charlie, with a cargo of sprogs making their operational début.

"Hardly knew him, sorry to say."

"Often the way," Adam remarked.

"You take care, Wing-Commander."

"You too, Herman." When O-Orange had touched down at a minute or so after one o'clock that morning the American had button-holed Adam. Having said barely a word on the return trip the floodgates had opened.

'Why the heck didn't you guys open fire on that fighter?'

Adam had met his eye.

'He was out of the range of our Brownings. Your countrymen in the 'Fighting Eighth' have fifty calibre heavy machine guns in their kites, we've only got rifle-calibre point three-oh-threes, but that's another story. The fighter was well out of the effective range of our guns.' He had gone on to explain that his gunners were under strict orders never open fire on a fighter unless it looked like it was about to attack them, or had already attacked them. 'And besides, it wasn't our turn.'

'It wasn't your turn for what?' Jablonski had asked, baffled.

Adam had summoned all his reserves of patience, spoken with an exaggerated slow patience. As if he was speaking to a dim-witted child.

'To get shot down, Herman.'

This had stunned Jablonski into silence. Only

later, as an afterthought did the big American remember to ask if they had any idea where O-Orange's bombs had actually fallen in the Berlin area.

'Oh yes,' Ben had confirmed, casually. 'We've got some idea.'

'But it's a secret or something, yeah?'

'Good lord no, old chap!' The navigator had smiled. 'If you're really interested, I'd hazard a guess we bombed somewhere in either the Moabit or Tiergarten Districts. Give or take a mile or two. Or maybe, three.'

Even as Herman Jablonski was driven away the Operations Room teleprinter was working overtime. In a few days the new moon would be ascendant, banishing the Main Force from the German night. Time was desperately short and much great work remained unfinished. The initial call to readiness did not specify a target, but the fuel and bomb loads promised somewhere distant and dangerous, possibly Berlin again. Adam had immediately called his Flight Commanders to an impromptu council of war. Peter Tilliard arrived first.

"The BBC have just said forty-one kites are missing, sir," he commented, depositing himself in the chair his CO indicated.

"About par for the course."

"Shame about Mick."

Mac knocked at the door and entered. Flight-Lieutenant Henry Barlow, the latest acting commander of B Flight followed him into the room.

"Thanks for dropping what you were doing, chaps," Adam kicked off as soon as everybody had settled. "I won't beat about the bush. Until the last two ops the Squadron had had a good run. This last week the odds seem to have caught up with us. There's no point getting downhearted about it. These things happen. The test of the best squadrons isn't whether or not they take the same knocks as everybody else, it's whether they can take those knocks and maintain their operational effectiveness. I am determined that 647 Squadron will maintain its operational effectiveness. Come what may."

The three officers sitting in a semi-circle in front of his desk nodded.

"The way I see it," Adam continued. "It is up to us to take a strong line. Lead from the front, show the chaps the way." He spoke with a grim resolve and his purposefulness was mirrored in his Flight Commanders' faces. He paused when there was a new knock at the door. "Come!" A WAAF entered, saluted and handed Adam a note.

"Thank you." Adam glanced at the note. "Halifax Force and all available Lancs to Leipzig," he announced. When the meeting broke up he asked Barlow to stay behind. "Sorry you've been dropped in the deep end like this, Henry."

The stocky, barrel-chested South African half-smiled, sadly.

"Can't be helped, sir."

"It may not be for too long," Adam said bluntly. "It's no reflection on you, Henry. But what with the expansion of the Squadron and the fact we've lost both Barney Knight and Mick Ferris in quick succession, I shall be pressing Group for an old hand. Your time will come."

Barlow tried valiantly, but failed to hide his

disappointment.

"Oh, I see, sir."

"As I say, Henry. Your turn will come."

Adam watched him go, cursed inwardly. Group Captain Alexander had put his foot down. It seemed the Deputy AOC had indicated to him that had Ferris not been advanced, an old lag from outside would have been forthcoming. The Old Man, not a great admirer of Barlow's - the gregarious Springbok was infamous both for his drinking exploits in the company of Mick Ferris and the cavalier way he flew a Lancaster - had been adamant.

'You've said it yourself often enough, Adam,' the Station Master had reminded him, brusquely. 'We need all the experience we can get!'

Adam was perfectly happy to promote Barlow. The man was a good sort, another pure bred warrior. However, it was not to be and there was no time to brood: Leipzig now awaited the pleasure of the Main Force.

Last night the defenders had inflicted another decimation on the Lancaster Force. The Chief's response was to despatch the Main Force even deeper into the German hinterland.

Chapter 5

Friday 3rd December, 1943
RAF Ansham Wolds, Lincolnshire

Suzy's letter was waiting for him when Tilliard got back from flight testing S-Sugar. He hurried back to his room to open the envelope in private. It was over a week, nine days, since he had received a letter from her and her silence had worried him.

Suzy's voice, bright and optimistic spoke to him from the page.

> *My Darling Peter,*
>
> *Oh, you clever, clever man! Your own Flight and a promotion. Squadron Leader! Squadron Leader Peter Tilliard. Oh, I'm so, so proud of you. You must be so pleased. And, I should imagine, so busy. When I heard the news I was so excited. I read your letter over and over again. I didn't take it in at first. I know you'll make a tremendous success of it!*
>
> *I've been very bad and not written to you. I get at least one letter most days from you which just makes me feel even more guilty. I promise I will make it up to you. Somehow.*
>
> *Now. My news. I'm to be posted back to 1 Group as a "de-briefer". I don't know which station yet, but obviously it won't be Ansham Wolds because I was a "ranker" there. I'm here in Shrewsbury for at least another week, they've laid on some extra*

classes for "the lucky ones" who are going off to Bomber Command.

After that, I'll probably spend most of my leave with mother and father (mother will make a dreadful fuss of me and it'll probably do me good, help me to get well again). When I know where I'm to be posted, we can arrange to meet and get to know each other again. That will be such fun, darling! Until then, I know how busy you must be and I don't want to be a "distraction". Things will be much simpler in future, us both being commissioned and so forth, and hopefully posted not that far from each other.

I love you and miss you, Suzy

"There you are!" Jack Gordon declared, barging into the room, stooping to drag his escape kit from beneath his cot. The rucksack scraped on the floor, heavily, and the Australian grunted with exertion.

"It looks like Suzy's coming back to Lincolnshire as a de-briefer," Tilliard informed him, not looking up.

"You're a lucky, lucky beggar!"

"She's planning to spend her leave with her people before she comes back up here."

Jack sat down heavily on his cot, fixed his friend with an amused, whimsical gaze. He shook his head slowly.

"Go on then?"

Tilliard blinked at him. "Go on what?" He inquired, irritably.

"Ask Uncle Jack what he'd do if he was you, of course!"

"I know I'm going to regret this," Tilliard muttered. "What would you do?"

The Australian grinned roguishly, slapped his knee. "Invite myself into the bosom of the lovely Suzy's family."

"I couldn't possibly!"

"If you really loved the girl you would."

Tilliard bit his tongue. Whether or not he 'really' loved Suzy was not at issue. He had no intention of inviting himself 'into the bosom' of Suzy's family. It was not on. Not done. Regardless of what pretext he might manufacture he was not going to descend unannounced on his future in-laws.

"Look," his navigator went on, only to be cut off in mid-flow.

"No, no!" Tilliard snapped, allowing his impatience to get the better of him. "The last thing Suzy would want me to do is to go blundering in upsetting the applecart, putting up a black with her people. No, it won't do!"

Jack chuckled. "Have it your own way, sport."

This said, he kicked off his shoes and lay down on his cot. There were the pre-op rituals to be observed. Peter Tilliard might let the lovely Suzy occupy his thoughts before the off but Jack Gordon was going to empty his mind, doze for half-an-hour before dressing for work and getting the show on the road. Until then there was no point wasting time or energy worrying about tonight's op. Leipzig was not going anywhere.

Unfortunately, Leipzig would still be there when he woke up.

Chapter 6

Friday 3rd December, 1943
Ansham Wolds, Lincolnshire

The first Lancasters roared overhead as Eleanor walked the children down the hill, through the woods to the Gatekeeper's Lodge. The light was fading fast.

Emerging into the scrub and weed-infested clearing that had once been the immaculate lawn below Ansham Hall, Eleanor stopped, watched the bombers swooping over the crumbling, gothic ruin of the old mansion. One by one the Lancasters flew across the valley, swung into a slow, climbing turn to the south, their navigation lights winking brightly in the gathering gloom. The evening was clear, hardly a breath of wind ruffled the face of the land, and high in the eastern sky the first stars twinkled.

The Lancasters were climbing in a long, endless chain over the high wold. It was impossible to be untouched by the spectacle, to be unmoved by the sound and fury of the bombers setting off for Germany. There had been a time when Eleanor had let it pass her by, pretended it was nothing to do with her and that she was somehow uninvolved, neutral. So much had changed since then. Her world had spun off its old axis, and sent her whirling wildly into a new, strange, exciting and utterly unexpected orbit.

Eleanor shivered. It was going to be a frosty night. When she got home she would build the fire in the parlour high, warm the house through, and put extra blankets on all the beds. The Rector reported the Lancasters had raided Berlin again last night 'in great strength'; and that over forty aircraft had failed to return. They had not dwelt on the subject. Simon had asked after her father, apologised for not having called to welcome him to the village, promised to visit the next day. Eleanor had advised him to stay indoors. The Rector had gone down with a cold and developed a racking, bronchial cough. The last thing she wanted him to do was to risk exacerbating his symptoms.

"I've explained to father that he's not the only invalid in Ansham at the moment. You must take care of yourself, Simon," she chided him. "Otherwise, I'm going to end up nursing two patients."

"One is quite enough," agreed the Rector, sneezing. "I shall see how I feel tomorrow. How is your father today?"

"I think he's got over the journey, now."

When he had arrived at the cottage late on Wednesday afternoon Eleanor had been deeply shocked at the deterioration in her father. He was hollow-eyed, ashen and enfeebled. Ben Hardiman almost had to carry him inside. But this morning after a day in bed a little of his strength had returned. The old man had seemed much more himself. Whereas, on Thursday he had meekly submitted to her fussing, today he had politely, firmly insisted that he was far from helpless and would be perfectly all right on his own.

Johnny and Emmy followed their mother's stare, tracking the progress of the bombers across the darkening skies. It was only when her daughter tugged at her hand that Eleanor remembered they ought to be making their way home.

At home she found her father dozing in front of a smouldering hearth, a book on his lap. She paused, spared him a fond look, placed a light kiss on his grey brow and set about stoking up the fire.

"I must have dropped off," yawned the old man, blinking at her in the half-light.

"You look much better today," Eleanor said, glancing up from arranging fresh wood on top of the re-awakened embers.

"I feel infinitely better for being here," her father replied, his tone heartfelt. "Oh, a registered letter came for you this afternoon. I left it on the kitchen table."

Eleanor focussed on raking the grate. The letter would be from the Magistrate's Clerk, Mr Thompson, in Thurlby. No doubt taking her to task for her inability to present herself before the bench on Wednesday afternoon. She had written apologising, explaining that she was anticipating the arrival in Ansham Wolds of her invalid father, that there were preparations to make, and of course, she could not simply abandon the village school. She had asked if she could attend another day. The Rector had added his own note, craving the Justice's indulgence.

"Your Aunt Lillian means well," her father was saying. "But I can't pretend it was an ideal situation in Wimbledon. I think she was secretly quite glad to get me off her hands. It's so quiet here..." He was interrupted by the passage of a Lancaster hurtling low over the chimney of the

Gatekeeper's Lodge. The windows rattled, the thunder of four straining Merlins drowned out his frail voice. "Apart from young Chantrey's damned heavies," he laughed. "As I was saying. Most of the time it is so quiet here. Very restful, such a nice change from London."

"I shall make a pot of tea," Eleanor announced, brushing a tear from her eye as she rose to her feet. "I thought we'd have game stew tonight. Or would you rather have something more easily digestible? Soup, perhaps?"

"Oh, proper food, I think, my dear," he retorted, defiantly. "But small measures for me, please," he added, in recognition of his dwindling appetite.

In the kitchen Eleanor stared at the brown envelope on the table for some seconds, then, deciding to hear the worst sooner rather than later, slit open the flap with a dinner knife.

She began to read.

Blinked in confusion, and read on.

"I don't understand…" She murmured, out aloud.

The Chambers
Magistrate's Court
Lindum Place
Thurlby-le-Wold
Lincolnshire

1st December, 1943

Dear Mrs Grafton,
    I am in receipt of your letter regarding your village and family

duties in Ansham Wolds, and also a supporting note from the Rev Naismith-Parry. I am also in receipt of an undertaking from another third party who has asked to remain anonymous at this time, standing surety for any costs your non-attendance at today's proceedings may occasion, and in respect of any fine which may be deemed appropriate if and when your case is heard, and a decision forthcoming.

 I am obliged to inform you that charges relating to two separate infringements of blackout regulations [Section 2, paras II, IV and IX of the Act apply] stand against your name. However, I fear there has been some misunderstanding in the matter of your obligation to appear before this Bench. I have written to the Chairman of the Ansham Wolds Air Raid Precautions Committee, Mr E.W. Rowbotham, to remind him that unless the infraction of the above regulations is liable to lead to a criminal case, the personal attendance of a defendant is not required under the Act. I am informed that Mr E.W. Rowbotham mistakenly notified you that attendance to answer the charges was obligatory, and I apologise if this has caused you undue worry.

    May I suggest that in due course, assuming you wish to contest matters, you submit any comments you wish to make to the Bench in writing, not later than 19th January, 1944, so that the Bench can consider the complaint of the Ansham Wolds ARP Committee when it next sits on Thursday 20th January.

    Your obedient servant,
      H.R. Thompson
    Clerk to the Justices.

"Oh, Adam..." She sighed, the weight of the world lifting off her shoulders. He should not have done it. He had done enough for her already; compelled her to cast off her mourning, given her back her father and restored her belief in the rightness of things. And now this. But he should not have done it. "Oh, Adam," she whispered, shaking her head, folding away the letter. "Whatever will I do with you..."

Much later, after they had eaten, Eleanor cleared away the plates and joined her father in the parlour. The children were in bed and the sky quiet. The old man had picked at his meal, nibbled what little he could and given in. The fire blazed high in the hearth, bathing the father and daughter in its heat.

"It sounded like quite a show tonight," the old man observed, viewing his daughter obliquely as she smoothed down her frock, and made herself comfortable in the chair opposite him. Eleanor looked up, smiled as she picked up her knitting needles and wool. The old man's expression became one of wry curiosity when he saw what she was knitting. His daughter said nothing for a while. The needles clicked and she counted stitches, silently to herself.

"Baby things," she offered, pointedly not volunteering further explanation.

"Oh," murmured her father, uncomfortably, not knowing how to interpret this. Eleanor was her mother's daughter in more ways than one, not a woman to be tied down by convention.

Eleanor laughed gently.

"Your face is a picture, father," she told him. "I said I'd do some things for Kate McDonald. Squadron Leader McDonald's wife. She's expecting her first baby in March. I had some of Johnny and Emmy's old woollens, so I unpicked enough wool to make a start. It's funny, I used to hate knitting, but now I've started again, it's rather fun. Quite relaxing."

"Your mother was never one for darning socks and the like," her father recollected.

"No," Eleanor concurred. Her mother had always had a housekeeper to attend to those things and a nanny to keep her offspring spick and span. As soon as she and her brother were old enough they were packed off to boarding schools. Eleanor had rejected her mother's way and latterly, forgiven her father for his part in her cold, sometimes loveless childhood. It was all past. Gone forever. Best forgotten.

"Do we know where Chantrey's heavies went to

last night, by the way?" Asked her father. "I didn't get around to turning on the wireless."

"Berlin, according to the Rector."

"Again?"

"Yes."

The old man sighed, resignedly. The Lancasters were faraway, flying into battle between the icy gales of winter and some part of Eleanor's soul now flew with them.

"I wonder where it is tonight?" He thought out aloud.

"We'll hear all about it tomorrow."

"And take it all for granted."

Eleanor stopped knitting.

"No, I don't think I shall ever be able to do that."

The old man kept his thoughts to himself. Too many people had long ago taken the war with the cities for granted. The inevitability of the campaign had slowly crept up on them over the last three years until now it was accepted as a sort of *sine qua non*. It seemed sometimes as if Bomber Command had been the sword bearer of all their hopes from the very outset.

Eleanor resumed her knitting, soon she was engrossed.

Her father let his thoughts roam. He was old-fashioned enough to still believe that the manner in which nations fought their wars - how they behaved in their darkest hour - was the truest expression of their underlying character. Bomber Command was, in Shakespearean parlance, England and everything that was England, at war. It was everything that was best and it was everything that was worst in the English. Would future generations remember that Bomber Command and its new, terrible Main Force could never have grown to maturity other than in the aftermath of the Luftwaffe's onslaught on British cities in the second winter of the war? He doubted it. Only the British truly understood righteous anger and Bomber Command was its logical manifestation…

Britain had not wanted war. In the early years Germany had heaped humiliation upon humiliation on Britain. At one stage Britain had stood alone with the evil tide of Nazism lapping at its beleaguered shores. Now, in cold blood, Bomber Command was exacting retribution and the reasons why had very little to do with the 'main aim', less still to do with the grand strategy of the Allies. Shakespeare would have understood what was going on and why. *'Caesar's spirit, ranging for revenge'* the Bard would have explained, *'came hot from hell, shall in these confines, with a monarch's voice cry Havoc! And let slip the dogs of war; that this foul deed shall smell above the earth with carrion men, groaning for burial…'* Twice in living memory Greater Germany had plunged the British people into World war. Never ever again. Bomber Command was wrecking Germany from end to end and the British people drew immense strength from the knowledge. True, there were a few dissenting voices, but the great mass of ordinary men and women in the street were wholly behind the bombing.

The Battle of Berlin was the battle for Germany. Yes, Shakespeare would have understood. It took a medieval mind to understand these things, a mind touched with mysticism, an innate sense of time past, and a tacit acceptance that history flows through a nation like the blood in the veins of its people. Some things are immutable. Some things are simply meant to be. Tonight, the Main Force was flying the high roads to Germany; not in the name of strategy, but because it was its destiny...

Eleanor looked up from her knitting.

Seeing her father sleeping, she smiled.

All was well in her world.

Chapter 7

Saturday 4th December, 1943
RAF Ansham Wolds, Lincolnshire

The raid itself had been a success and had the bomber stream not strayed south over the defences of Frankfurt-am-Main on the way back, the victory would have been almost bloodless. Half the 24 heavies lost over Germany had fallen to the Frankfurt flak, with many of the casualties coming from the lower-flying Halifaxes.

B Flight's new commander arrived at Ansham Wolds that morning and wasted no time in presenting himself to his CO.

"Squadron Leader Nicholson, sir," said the newcomer as hands were shaken. He passed over his orders, and viewed the drab, chilly office with an impatient, haughty eye.

Adam dropped behind his desk, glanced cursorily at the paperwork.

'Squadron Leader R.M. Nicholson, DFC, shall report to the Air Officer Commanding No. 647 (Heavy Bomber) Squadron at 12:00 hours, 4th December. There to assume the duties of Deputy Squadron Commander, and Flight Commander at the discretion of the OC said Squadron...'

Adam scowled. Nobody at Group had had the courtesy to let him know Nicholson had been posted to Ansham Wolds as his second-in-command.

"It is Bob, isn't it?"
"Yes, sir."

"Take a pew, Bob."

"Thank you, sir."

Adam knew very little about Nicholson but what little he did know did not inspire confidence: a tour on Stirlings and a spell on the AOC's personal staff at Bawtry Hall was hardly the ideal preparation for a tour on Lancasters. The two men had previously only met in passing.

"How many hours on Lancs have you got, Bob?" He inquired, determined to make the best of things.

"None, sir," Nicholson drawled. His tone implied that he did not foresee this being a problem. To the contrary, he seemed rather proud of himself. "I'm a Stirling man."

A Stirling man!

Adam pursed his lips, tried not to frown. "I see," he grunted. "And how long have you been away from ops?"

"About a year, sir."

About a year!

"A year?"

"Yes, sir," Nicholson confirmed, airily. "I'm sure I'll soon get the hang of things again. Things can't have changed that much while I've been away."

Things can't have changed that much!

Momentarily, Adam looked at the new man in blank, uncomprehending astonishment. He did not know which was the more galling; the smug, complacent grin on the newcomer's face or the crassness of the system that had sent him to Ansham Wolds in the first place.

"Eton or Harrow?" He asked, sourly.

"Eton, actually," Nicholson replied, the grin fading. "Why do you ask, sir?"

"Idle curiosity, that's all," Adam assured him. Coincidentally, the Deputy AOC was an old Etonian. "I'm a Charterhouse man myself. You probably knew Barney Knight, then?"

"Only vaguely, he was a year or two below me. A fine fellow."

Adam nodded, reached for the phone. He dialled the station switchboard, asked to be put through to the Adjutant. There was a short delay. Tom Villiers came on the line.

"Tom, can you send out search parties for Mac and Peter Tilliard, ask them to report to my room, please. Yes, soonest. Thank you." He replaced the receiver, pulled his cigarette case from his tunic pocket, offered it to Nicholson.

"I don't, sir," said the other, primly.

"Not a teetotaller as well, I hope!" Adam grimaced, attempting to lighten the atmosphere, establish some kind of rapport. The remark fell on arid, stony ground.

"Er, yes. As it happens. I take the view that drinking and flying don't mix, sir."

Inwardly, Adam permitted himself a groan: the man had never flown a Lancaster; had no recent operational experience, and; worse, he was a prig. And this was the man Group had sent to Ansham Wolds to replace him!

To command his Squadron in due course!

"Oh well," Adam countered. "Each to his own, what? Anyway, before the others arrive a few words to the wise, Bob."

Nicholson leaned towards him, a picture of respectful attentiveness.

Adam hurried on.

"The first thing you've got to do is convert to Lancs. On this Squadron nobody flies ops until they've satisfied *me* that they're up to it."

"I shall be up to it in no time sharp," announced the other man. "A few circuits and bumps should do it."

"Possibly. However, just so there's no misunderstanding about this, Bob," Adam stressed. "You don't fly ops until I give you the all clear."

"Of course not, sir."

"Second. Crew selection. You can take your pick from our pool of odd sods, but I won't have you, or any other chap for that matter, breaking up existing crews."

"Wouldn't dream of it."

Adam wondered if Nicholson was paying the slightest notice to a single word he was saying.

"Talk to Mac and Peter, do a couple of ops as a passenger. Your senior pilot, Henry Barlow has got about twenty ops under his belt. Bit of a rough diamond, I'm bound to say. But for all that he's a good man. A damned good man. A chap with his heart in the right place. If I were you I wouldn't be afraid to listen to his advice."

Nicholson coughed.

"I have my own way of doing things, sir."

"So do I, Bob," Adam rapped. "And this is *my* Squadron."

"Sorry, sir. I just meant..."

"Bob, by your own admission you're a Stirling man on a Lancaster squadron with no current operational experience. Take it from me, this is not the time to be doing things *your* way. Do I make myself clear?"

Nicholson glared back at him. There was an awkward pause.

"Yes, sir."

Stand down was confirmed at 10:45. Low, sullen cloud hung over the airfield, ruling out flying for the rest of the day. However, while A and C Flights' crews were stood down, Squadron Leader Nicholson posted an order summoning B Flight to a 'briefing' at 14:00 hours. Initially, he had requested that as 647 Squadron's new second-in-command he be formally introduced to all the crews that afternoon but Adam had put his foot down.

"The crews have been over Germany the last two nights," he reminded him, barely able to contain his exasperation. "Your Flight is your domain. If the other Flight Commanders elect to stand down their crews that is their prerogative. They are responsible to me for the operational proficiency and the moral of their crews, as you are for your crews."

Mac had taken the news that his brief tenure as deputy Squadron Commander was over with the quiet fortitude of one who has many times, endured greater setbacks. However, both he and Peter Tilliard were aghast to discover Nicholson had never flown a Lancaster.

'We'll look after you,' Peter Tilliard assured the new man, offering to personally oversee his conversion.

'Please don't concern yourself,' Nicholson had declared. 'I'm sure I shall be all right. I'll gen up on the manual and get one of my pilots to show me around the cockpit.'

Mac had thrown an anxious look in the

direction of his CO.

'Peter came to us via the HCU at Lindholme,' the Scot told the newcomer. 'He'll get you converted in no time.'

Tilliard had nodded vigorously.

'Won't hear of it!' Nicholson retorted, curtly. 'I should imagine you chaps have got enough on your plates as it is.'

When Adam went in search of Group Captain Alexander aircrew were streaming purposefully down to the main gates of the station to catch the mid-afternoon buses, one to Grimsby and Cleethorpes, others to Scunthorpe via Brigg and Broughton. The Group Captain was walking Rufus beyond the watchtower.

"Bloody good prang last night," boomed the Old Man when Adam finally caught up with him. "Most of our chaps seem to have brought back prints within a mile or two of the AP. Damned good show! So, what's the new man like?"

They had spoken only in passing about Nicholson's arrival. Adam had promised to report back properly later. He broke the bad news as gently as possible.

"A bit odd."

"Oh. In what way? They think he's the bee's knees at Group."

"I'm sure they do, sir." Adam was trying hard to give Nicholson the benefit of the doubt. First impressions were fickle things. The man deserved a chance to prove himself.

"Three Group man, originally, wasn't he?"

Rufus quartered the ground ahead of them, weaving from side to side, pausing occasionally to sniff the air.

"A Stirling man, sir. Unfortunately, no time on Lancs."

The Station Master halted abruptly.

"None at all?"

"None. And he hasn't flown ops for a year."

"You're joking?"

"Afraid not, sir."

Alexander exploded.

"What on earth do they think they're doing sending him here!"

Adam could not think of anything positive to say, so he said nothing. The older man marched on, snorting his displeasure. Rufus looked at him warily and decided to keep his distance.

When a fine, cold drizzle began to descend they headed back towards civilisation.

"Pay my respects to the Prof. I must pop down to see him one day soon."

"You're welcome to come with me, sir. I was planning to put my head around the door this evening."

"Another day, perhaps. I'm sure you've got things to discuss with Eleanor."

Despite himself, Adam chuckled.

"Quite so, sir."

Chapter 8

Saturday 4th December, 1943
The Gatekeeper's Lodge, Ansham Wolds, Lincolnshire

Eleanor heard the car in the lane. She was silhouetted in the doorway as Adam clambered stiffly to his feet, waved and walked towards her in the falling rain.

The man hoped his face was hidden in the darkness, his guilt masked. He halted before the woman, unable to cloak his inner unease. It was the first time he had visited the cottage, or dared to face Eleanor since engineering the Prof's trip up to Lincolnshire. The letters that Tom Villiers – drawing on his experience in his previous life as a country solicitor - had drafted on his behalf to the village ARP Committee and to the Clerk to the Magistrates in Thurlby would have hit their marks in the last few days, also. How would she react? He half expected her to fly at him yet when their eyes met he knew all was well.

"Come here," Eleanor murmured, throwing her arms around his neck, pulling him close against her with a happy sigh.

Adam swept her up in his arms, hugged her tight, buried his face in her hair. They held each other for an eternity, swaying gently. The rain pattered softly on their shoulders but they were oblivious to it, lost in a world of their own, a world in which rain never fell.

Eleanor raised her head from his chest, her eyes

moist, glinting wetly in the half-light of the oil lamps burning lowly in the hallway.

"Kiss me," she breathed, lifting her mouth to his. Her lips were warm, soft against his. They kissed slowly, deeply until light-headed, reeling, they remembered themselves, stepped back, gazed one to the other. "Oh, I love you, Adam Chantrey," she declared, huskily in the gloom. "I love you so much!"

Adam's thoughts were spinning. Eleanor's nearness, the rawness of his feelings rocked his equilibrium, left him trembling. He tried to get a grip of himself. His throat was dry, constricted and his voice failed him. He gazed to her. Everything had changed, they had crossed a line that could never be uncrossed. He had been infatuated, fascinated by the woman from the start. Looking into her hazel brown eyes he ached for her, and knew that she ached for him, too. The realisation took his breath away.

Reading his thoughts, Eleanor put a finger to his lips.

"No. Don't say a word. Not a word, darling."

He shrugged, helplessly. He wanted to tell her that he loved her. Wanted to shout it aloud, shout it to the rooftops, shout it to the heavens but the words strangled in his throat.

"Not a single word," she repeated, smiling and sniffing back a tear.

Adam followed Eleanor into the cottage. In front of the fire he took her hands and she melted into his arms again, leaned against him.

"You've missed the children, again."

"Sorry."

Eleanor went up on tip toes, covered his mouth with hers, kissed him with a careless abandon that set Adam's senses racing, his spine tingling. His hunger for her was almost unbearable. He fought the urge to paw at her, maul her, rip at her clothes. The wanting was so strong, all-consuming, frightening. Somehow, he got a grip. Tenderly, he stepped back and held her at arm's length.

"I thought you'd be angry?"

Eleanor laughed, viewed him sympathetically. "Why ever would I be angry, darling?"

"Ah, well, yes," he muttered, avoiding her eye. "How is the Prof, by the way?"

"Tucked up in bed. Fast asleep."

"I ought to have called before. To pay my respects."

"And to visit me, I hope."

"Of course."

Eleanor brushed herself down, deftly adjusted the band in her hair. The fire in the hearth had burned low, the embers glowed in the grate. The man and the woman retreated into the shadows.

"What is it?" She asked, presently.

"Nothing." They were normal again, in control.

"We'd better not disturb father."

"No. We mustn't do that."

"Sit down. I'll make some cocoa."

Adam sat in the armchair by the fire, stared into the embers, contemplated the fates that had brought him here. He told himself he was not a free man but it did not help. He still felt torn, in the wrong. As if he was letting Eleanor down.

"Aren't we a pair?" Eleanor said, returning with the cocoa. She knelt on the rug by the hearth, her skirts spread around her. She looked up at him as she cradled her mug in her small, pale hands.

Adam tore his eyes away from the fire.

"I have this dream," he confessed. "It keeps coming back. Over and over again. It is the same dream every time, more or less. It always ends the same way. The kite's burning, diving out of control and I'm trapped. Centrifugal force and all that. Everything's on fire and there's nothing I can do about it. Nothing."

The resignation in his voice chilled Eleanor's heart.

"But it is *only* a dream, darling. A nightmare, that's all."

He shook his head.

"That's what I used to think. But lately, every time I fly an op I recognise another bit of the dream. It's as if every op brings me another step nearer the end of the dream."

Eleanor shivered.

"It's just a dream."

"I ought to have bought it a long time ago," he said very quietly, almost to himself. "I could have bought it two or three times since I met you. Easily. Very easily. I've been living on borrowed time for a long while now. So long in fact that I don't get afraid any more. Well, hardly ever. I see other kites going down, I look at the flak coming up towards me, the fires on the ground and none of it seems real. It's as if I'm looking at a newsreel of somebody else's war, as if I'm not even there. I've got so used to shutting things out, I suppose." He shook his head, steeled himself to seek out Eleanor's gaze. He had been reconciled to his death for a long time. Ever since the Wilhelmshaven disaster, truth be known. "I think, my love, that you are very much braver than me. But it's no use pretending things are normal, that I can promise you things. That I can promise you anything..."

Very deliberately, Eleanor rose to her feet and took the mug of cocoa from his hands. She placed it beside her own on the hearth and settled on his lap, curled up against him, sheltered in the circle of his arms.

"I don't care a fig for any of that, you stupid man," she sniffed, defiantly, blinking through the tears. "Not one fig!"

Chapter 9

Thursday 16th December, 1943
RAF Waltham Grange, Lincolnshire

Acting-Assistant Section Officer Suzy Mills was exhausted trying to keep up with the Operations Officer, a large, affable man with a long, ground-devouring stride.

"Stick close to me, today," Flight-Lieutenant Ramsey had told her, early that morning. "You've arrived on a good day. You'll soon get the hang of things. A lot of your duties will be to do with the logistical side. Getting the reports together, checking the returns to Group for typographical errors, making sure we don't let too many howlers through. That sort of thing. But on ops days you've really got to be on the ball. The sooner you can get yourself genned up the better. The chaps are much more forthcoming about what's what when there's a pretty face on hand. Especially, if they think you really know your stuff."

The Operations Officer had escorted Suzy on a whirlwind tour of Waltham Grange, taking in the Briefing Hall, watchtower, flight room, admin hut and of course, the Operations Room. She had been introduced to a bewildering number of people, among them the senior bombing, navigation and engineering officers, her new WAAF colleagues on the Operations Staff, the Intelligence Officer, and the Met Officer. Everybody was busy preparing for the coming raid. Semi-organized chaos reigned and the events of the day had merged into a blur, a fascinating, exhilarating blur.

"Bit of flap, today," Ramsey had explained enthusiastically, rubbing his hands together, smiling broadly. "We're on for Berlin tonight and it's another early start because there'll be a three-quarters moon later."

Around mid-day a boyish Squadron Leader materialised in the Operations Room. He seemed no older than Suzy herself, his face was pale, his eyes were a little sunken and his gaze never lingered on one place for more than a moment. She knew the signs, had seen them before. He was a man at the end of his tether, twitchy. The newcomer walked into the Met Officer's room. A minute later he had stalked out, looking neither to left nor right, bristling with anger.

"Squadron Leader Hamilton," the Ramsey had informed Suzy, very quietly, confidentially. "The acting CO. The Wingco went missing on the Leipzig show. There's fog forecast for this evening and the chaps are a bit ring rusty. A bit edgy. No ops now for a fortnight, you see. Not good for the nerves. Hammy's an excitable chap at the best of times. Best to keep out of his way when he's got a bee in his bonnet."

"I'm sorry," Suzy had stuttered, colouring in discomfort.

She was horrified to think that the hollow-eyed boy who had just stalked out of the Ops Room carried the whole crushing burden of commanding 388 Squadron on his slender shoulders.

"That was the CO?"

"Hammy, yes." Ramsey had narrowed his eyes, frowned. "Lovely chap, underneath. He just takes things a tad too much to heart, that's all. Salt of the earth. Everybody gets a bit brassed off from time to time. You'll get used to it. Take it from me." He changed the subject. "Coming from Ansham Wolds, you'll have come across the Wingco before last from around these parts, I dare say?"

"Er, Wing-Commander Chantrey?"

"That's the chap! The crews were sorry to see him go. Mind you, everybody on the non-flying side of things was scared stiff of him, he could be a holy terror with desk jockeys like us, but you don't mind a little thing like that when things are going swimmingly, what?"

"No, sir."

"Things have got a bit sticky since he left. Apart from Hammy and Clive Irving, not many of the chaps from those days are still around."

Suzy contemplated this.

Wing-Commander Chantrey had arrived at Ansham Wolds at the end of September, less than three months ago. In the Waafery the previous night she had cautiously inquired what Waltham Grange 'was like', specifically how '388 Squadron had been faring'. Her roommate, an older woman who came from Colchester, was sarcastic.

"Depends what you're used to, I suppose," the other woman had replied, "but if I were you I wouldn't go getting friendly with anybody on ops. Not the way things are going."

Suzy rather resented the way everybody she met at Waltham Grange seemed to take one look at her and automatically assume she was wet behind the ears. She had seen and heard things at Ansham Wolds that would make their hair stand on end.

And besides, this place had exactly the same sort of feel about it as Ansham Wolds in the days just before Wing-Commander Fulshawe committed suicide. Ansham Wolds's salvation had been the arrival of Wing-Commander Chantrey. Wing-Commander Chantrey had brought with him a reputation on ops second to none and most of the crews were in awe of him from the outset. Here at Waltham Grange, salvation lay in the hands of poor "Hammy" Hamilton. She shivered, involuntarily.

"Are you all right?" Ramsey asked.

"Yes, sir."

"Oh. You looked a bit peaky just then."

"I'm okay, sir. Honestly."

Tonight the Main Force was flying the direct route to the Big City.

"Any other route and the moon will be up before the chaps reach Berlin," Ramsey remarked. "We think most of the night fighter fields will be fogged-in but there's no point taking too many risks. The route back is interesting. After the chaps have bombed they're to turn north-east, then when they're clear of the Berlin defended zone, north-west over Denmark. That'll put a bit of distance between them and the fighters by the time the moon's fully up." Over Berlin the Pathfinders would employ the normal 'Berlin Method'. "At the beginning of the attack the 'specials' will put down green TIs. Then the 'blind markers' will back up with reds. Once the openers have done their bit, the backers-up will carry on the good work. Of course, if there's ten-tenths over the target, again, it'll be Sky Markers all round!"

Suzy was guiltily enjoying her ring-side seat at

the party. The Operations Officer was a mine of information. "Trouble is, we haven't got any recce photographs of the damage we've done in Berlin. Not for want of trying, I'm told."

"So, how do we know if we've hit anything at all, sir?" She asked, a little incredulously.

It seemed the obvious question. It had never occurred to her that, four weeks into the campaign against the German capital, Command still did not have a shred of photographic evidence that a single bomb load had actually fallen on Berlin.

Ramsey was untroubled by the fact. It was a detail. The crews knew when they had fired a city. They knew when they had flown over clouds painted red like mile upon mile of blood-soaked cotton wool. There was no doubt whatsoever that huge areas of the Big City had been laid waste.

"Spies, diplomatic contacts. Reports in the foreign press. Who knows? Recce photos notwithstanding, the feeling at Group is that we should just press on. You know, keep on repeating the medicine. Command must feel the same way because the AP is pretty well slap bang in the middle of the city again tonight."

388 Squadron's Lancasters began taking off at four o'clock that afternoon. As the controller reported each aircraft safely airborne, the Operations Staff chalked it up on the wall. Suzy watched, listened and quickly learned. Her short period of training was over; in the early hours of the morning she would be debriefing men who had looked death in the eye and survived.

Outside low cloud loomed over Lincolnshire. The portent of disaster. She wondered if Peter was flying tonight.

Around dusk she always thought about Peter Tilliard.

Chapter 10

Thursday 16th December, 1943
Lancaster B-Beer, 20 miles NNE of Cromer

B-Beer climbed out of the cloud over the North Sea. Behind the Lancaster the setting sun illuminated the western horizon and lit the way to the east. Other heavies ascended into clear air below B-Beer, more were visible up ahead, clawing for height.

Jack Gordon listened to the gunners chattering over the intercom. They were complaining about the sunset, exchanging nervy quips about the brightness 'hurting' their eyes. He stayed put in the darkness of the navigator's alcove, deep inside the fuselage. He wanted a series of good *Gee* fixes before the set was jammed.

He heard Peter Tilliard's voice slice through the gunners' banter.

"Pilot to crew."

These days Peter radiated a calm authority that instantly seized a man's attention and instilled unquestioning confidence. The transformation in him in the two months Jack had known him was immense. He had got over losing his first crew, proved to everybody, and most importantly to himself, that he was the sort of chap who 'pressed on'. Nobody questioned his right to have C Flight. Nobody in the land of the living, anyway.

"That's enough chat for now, chaps," Tilliard decided. "Pilot to navigator. How far are we out to sea, Jack?"

"Navigator to pilot. Plenty, Skipper."

"Right ho. Pilot to gunners. Test you guns please, over."

The bomber shook to the recoil of its .303 Browning machine guns.

"Pilot to navigator. Looks like ten-tenths from horizon to horizon up ahead, Jack. If you've not already done it, it might be an idea to warm up the *H2S* set before we cross the enemy coast."

"Roger, Skipper. We want to start *Windowing* in about ten minutes, by the way."

"Pilot to bomb-aimer. Did you hear that, Billy?" Tilliard inquired. The intercom hissed.

Billy Campbell's young voice crackled over the line. "Start *Windowing* in one-oh minutes, Skipper!"

Jack Gordon noted the time on his pad. He would remind both his pilot, and the bomb-aimer to commence *Windowing* in exactly ten minutes time. His left knee pressed against the bulging side of his escape kit. The rucksack got fuller with every op.

'What you got in there, mate?' Dave Wrigley, the chain-smoking, permanently dishevelled rear gunner continually asked. 'The bloody kitchen sink, or what?'

'Snow White and the Seven Bogging Dwarfs!' He would retort. 'What do you bloody think I've got in there?'

'The bloody kitchen sink, mate!'

'Ha, bloody, ha!'

A chap could not be too careful when it came to his escape kit. Not when he had responsibilities and other people to think about; Nancy Bowman, for example. The lovely Nancy. Jack had got himself into a very, very deep hole with Nancy

Bowman, the youngest daughter of the landlord of the *Hare and Hounds*. Nancy was blond, buxom, warm-hearted and utterly devoted to him, everything a man could want or hope for in a woman. She was also with child. *His* child. Earlier that afternoon he had come clean with Peter. Explained his predicament, and asked his advice. Peter was a decent fellow, he would know what to do for the best.

'You must marry the girl, Jack!'

'Oh, you think so?'

'You MUST!'

'Oh.'

The odd thing was that until Peter had mentioned marriage Jack had not even considered it. Not seriously. Yet no sooner had the word been broached than he realised that it was not only the obvious thing to do, but that he really had no other choice. What was more, the idea tickled him pink.

'Look, old man,' Peter Tilliard had continued, not wholly convinced that he was preaching to the converted. 'Nancy thinks the world of you and any fool can see that you're absolutely besotted with her. You must marry her! The sooner the better!'

His friend's vehemence had shaken Jack out of his paralysis, a shocked paralysis which had ensnared him the moment Nancy had broken 'her' news to him the previous weekend. There was of course, a problem; the father of the prospective bride. Bill Bowman, normally a man of limitless bonhomie had in his past life been a redoubtable, much feared fairground pugilist and was not a man to be trifled with.

'How am I going to face Bill, though?'

'Simple. Man to man. You ask him for his daughter's hand in marriage.'

'Oh, right!' Jack had protested. 'Then what do I do, you know, after I get out of hospital?'

'Don't be such an ass, Jack! If you won't break the news to Bill, I will!' His friend had become a little agitated at this stage. Angry, in fact. 'Damn it, Jack! The Bowmans treat you like the prodigal returned, a member of the family. You ought to be ashamed of yourself!'

'It was a mistake, okay!'

'That's as maybe. Fortunately, for you, it was with a lovely girl who will make you an equally lovely wife. As soon that is, as you pluck up the courage to do the right thing! The decent thing!'

'Christ, Peter,' Jack had complained. 'You're beginning to sound like my old dad. It's not as if you and Suzy haven't played doctors and nurses!'

Peter Tilliard had stiffened, scowled wordlessly.

Jack had instantly caught himself, apologised profusely. He had over-stepped the mark. Had their situations been reversed, Peter Tilliard would not have needed to have been reminded what 'the right thing to do' was. He would have known, intuitively. Jack had held up his hands.

'Forget I said that. Sorry.'

'Already forgotten, Jack.'

'Did you mean it when you said you'd help me break the news to Bill?'

'Tomorrow. We'll nip down to Kingston Magna tomorrow.'

Tomorrow they might both be dead. Tomorrow would be soon enough to worry about the wrath of – as he had been in his fairground heyday - 'iron-fisted Billy' Bowman. Tonight he could face the night fighters and the Berlin flak with something approaching equanimity.

Jack Gordon stared at the fuzzy image on the *H2S* screen as the Norfolk coast slid off the scope. There were two sharp white contacts near the middle of the tube. Ships, fishing boats, perhaps. Coastal Command used *H2S* for hunting U-boats. Over water the apparatus effortlessly located objects as small as a U-boat's conning tower at ranges of twenty or thirty miles. If its magic eye had been as all-seeing over land they would have been laughing.

Laughing all the way to the victory parade.

Chapter 11

Thursday 16th December, 1943
RAF Ansham Wolds, Lincolnshire

The Reverend Poore found the Wingco in the Operations Room reading a two-day old copy of the Evening Standard. At his diffident approach the younger man glanced up.

"Our will to win is unshakable," Adam observed, ruefully.

This caught the Padre off guard.

"Ah, I should imagine so, yes," he agreed, haltingly. The CO had been in good form lately, if not a changed man then at least a rested, refreshed man. Everybody had benefited from the recent lull in operations.

"That's what Goebbels is telling Berliners, anyway."

"Oh, the *German* will to win is unshakable?"

"That's what Herr Goebbels says."

"Hardly an unimpeachable source, I'd suggest?"

"What? The *Standard* or Goebbels?"

The Reverend Poore was becoming accustomed to being the butt of the CO's little jokes. He regarded it as a compliment, a mark of respect. He had sensed from the start that he and the young tyro were kindred spirits united by their particular responsibilities to the crews.

"You wanted to see me, sir?"

"These films we've had lately?"

The Padre frowned. The base gymnasium served both as his church and a cinema. Most nights he organised a film show, sometimes two. He tried to get hold of recent, well-known films.

"Is there a problem, sir?"

"No, no, nothing like that. You're doing a dashed good job on the entertainments side of things, excellent for morale and so forth."

"But?"

"A few more musicals and some comedies would be just the ticket," Adam put to him. "The chaps get enough blood and thunder on ops without having Errol Flynn, Douglas Fairbanks and that nice Mr Coward ramming more of it down their throats every night. As I say, just a thought, Padre."

It was a thought that had also crossed the Reverend Poore's mind.

"It's not always easy to get, er, lighter material, I'm afraid, sir. But I shall endeavour to do my best, of course."

"Good man."

"Oddly enough, sir," the older man went on. "When I spoke to Mr. Nicholson earlier this afternoon he made exactly the same suggestion. About the film shows."

"Oh." This made a small puncture in the bubble of Adam's good humour. "Did he indeed?"

"Yes, sir."

"Oh, well," the younger man grunted. "Great minds thinking alike, and so on, what."

The Reverend Poore paused for thought. The Squadron's new second-in-command had – largely unwittingly - left a trail of outraged sensibilities and a deal of chaos in his wake. The man meant well but he was like a fish out of water at Ansham

Wolds, in danger of becoming a laughing stock. Outwardly, the Wingco stood four-square behind Bob Nicholson, but the Padre was only too well aware of the younger man's underlying exasperation with the newcomer.

"Mind you," Adam said, acidly. "Credit where credit's due. I'd never have thought of banning bicycles from the Mess! A corker, that one!"

The Padre recoiled, inwardly. It was said softly, too softly to carry beyond his ears. Nevertheless, it was the first time he had ever heard the CO openly disparage one of his officers. Bicycle racing in the Mess was an Ansham Wolds tradition - for all he knew it was a pursuit common throughout the Command - and last night there had been several races. One of A Flight's crews was transferring to the Pathfinders and there had been a party. During the festivities Squadron Leader Nicholson had been knocked down. Had he treated this indignity as a joke, got into the spirit of the occasion, he might have taken a giant stride towards gaining acceptance into the brotherhood of the crews. Instead, he had stood on his dignity, torn the offender off a strip and worse, threatened to put him on a charge. Peter Tilliard had stepped in, tried to smooth down ruffled feathers and acted as a peacemaker and save Nicholson from himself. To little or no avail. Consequently, the Squadron's second-in-command had diminished himself even further in the eyes of his fellows.

The Padre was tempted to say nothing but resisted the temptation. He had not come to Ansham Wolds to hide in a darkened room at the first sign of trouble.

"It's my impression that, upon reflection, Squadron Leader Nicholson regrets what happened yesterday as much as anybody, sir. Tempers fraying in the heat of the moment, and so on…"

Adam sighed, put down his paper.

"Where's that bloody dog of mine?" The Padre was paid to think the best of people. He was not. "I suppose I ought to take him for a walk before the bloody fog gets too thick!"

Chapter 12

Thursday 16th December, 1943
Lancaster B-Beer, 15 miles ESE of Den Helder

Tilliard's heart sank. One by one the flares drifted down, swinging on their parachutes, directly ahead. Fighter flares, two lines of them blowing in the wind three miles high over Holland. B-Beer droned on, far below her the clouds stretched as far as the eye could see in every direction.

"Pilot to gunners," he called, trying hard not to sound worried. "Fighter flares at twelve o'clock. Keep your wits about you, chaps. Over."

The first combat took place about five minutes later.

A multi-coloured plume of flame fell into the clouds, arcing down across the blackness in a long, slow curve. There was no tracer, no return fire. Just the flames of 100-octane and miscellaneous target indicators spewing into the blackness, a stricken Pathfinder falling to its doom in the skies of a foreign land many miles from home.

Jack Gordon's voice crackled over the intercom.

"Navigator to pilot. We're crossing the enemy coast, now. Over."

"Thank you, Jack," Peter Tilliard drawled, steeling himself. Another heavy was going down, this time several miles north of B-Beer's ground track. "Be a good chap and keep us tucked into the stream. It looks as if we might be batting on a bit of sticky wicket tonight. Over."

There was a pause. Then.

"I'll do my best, Skipper."

"Good man."

Beneath the canopy of the silent, neutral stars the Lancaster Force bored on across the Zuider Zee and into Germany. The fighters sniped at the flanks of the bomber stream, heavies succumbed with monotonous regularity. The route was marked by fighter flares. Mercifully, the clouds concealed the wrecks of the Lancasters burning far below on the plains of northern Germany.

Tilliard made no attempt to shut out his fear. Fear was good, fear sharpened reflexes, fear kept a man on the ball. No matter how bloody things got you had to carry on, trusting to your skills and to the fortunes of war.

North of Magdeburg Jack Gordon came on the intercom.

"Any chance of giving the weaving a rest for a minute, Skipper? The bloody *H2S* set's just started smoking and I'd like to get a couple of star sights before we reach the target."

Tilliard thought about it, briefly.

"Pilot to navigator. Let me know when you're in position, Jack."

He could feel the rest of the crew tense up but it could not be helped. There was no way Jack could get a reliable star fix while the aircraft was weaving erratically, sometimes violently across the sky. Without *H2S* and with no sight of the ground since leaving Ansham Wolds, B-Beer could be fifty miles off track.

"Navigator to pilot," Jack reported, tersely. "I'm in position. Ready when you are, Skipper."

"Don't hang about, Jack," Tilliard pleaded,

silently mouthing a prayer.

The Lancaster steadied on course, flew straight and level into the east.

"Combat astern at eight o'clock," shouted Dave Wrigley, excitedly. The normally taciturn rear-gunner's nerves were red raw tonight. "Range three to four miles. Heavy going down, now!"

B-Beer droned on.

In the south-east flak peppered the night. Somebody was lost.

Tilliard fought the urge to chivvy his navigator along. Jack knew what he was about, he needed no chivvying. He felt naked, the back of his neck tingled. The controls were rock steady under his hands.

"Come on, Jack!" He muttered under his breath, every sinew braced for instant, desperate evasive action. An age went by, seconds dragging like minutes.

"Navigator to pilot. Get weaving, Skipper!"

Tilliard heard Jack's voice, banked the bomber to the left, touched the rudder, let B-Beer drift off track.

"FIGHTER PORT!" Wrigley screamed. "CORKSCREW STARBOARD. NOW! NOW! NOW!"

Tilliard responded immediately, hurled the Lancaster into a near vertical bank to the right, stamped on the right rudder bar, and thrust the starboard throttles through the gate. B-Beer fell into space, her tortured airframe and Merlins crying out in protest.

"FOLLOWING US DOWN! GO PORT! NOW! NOW!"

Instantly he hauled the controls to the left with

every ounce of strength in his body. The nose rose, the aircraft juddered on the point of a stall, instinctively he jammed the port throttles hard up against their stops. B-Beer reared into a gut-wrenching turn to port.

"FIGHTER ATTACKING! GO STARBOARD! NOW! NOW!"

Tilliard had already applied maximum opposite aileron, anticipating the fighter would try to turn inside them. Behind him a body was thrown across the fuselage, first one way then the other, thudding, groaning. Tracer flashed over his head. B-Beer shuddered as 20 millimetre cannon shells ripped into her. The cockpit filled with the stench of burnt cordite. There was an explosion behind him, the bomber lurched sideways. The control column was momentarily wrenched from his hands.

The Lancaster dived headlong.

"HE'S COMING ROUND AGAIN! CORKSCREW STARBOARD! NOW! NOW!"

Tilliard grabbed the controls, stood the heavy on its starboard wingtip, yanked back on the right-hand throttles, kicked hard at the rudder bar. B-Beer screamed into the dive. Steeper and steeper, faster and faster she fell.

All thoughts of the fighter were suddenly forgotten.

The aircraft was out of control.

Tilliard stood in his seat, hauled back on the controls with all his might. The slipstream thundered, the blood pounded in his temples. The controls seemed frozen, immovable in his hands. No matter how hard he pulled the Lancaster continued to rush earthward, the airspeed indicator reeled off impossible numbers: 310…320…330…340…

The controls were coming back towards him.

He told himself it was already too late.

350…360…

B-Beer would shed her wings any moment, now. The Lancaster was shaking herself to pieces, every rivet straining. B-Beer plunged into the clouds.

"NO!"

Tilliard heard himself scream it. He was not yet ready to die. Tonight was not the night he was meant to die. If tonight was the night he would have known it, sensed it from the off. This was all wrong, unfair, unjust.

"NO!"

Chapter 13

Thursday 16th December, 1943
The Gatekeeper's Lodge, Ansham Wolds, Lincolnshire

With the children tucked up in bed Eleanor looked in on her father. He was asleep, grey and exhausted in the bed. A single candle by the bedside flickered. The doctor had come again that afternoon and prescribed laudanum. Eleanor sat in the rocking chair at the foot of the bed, pulled her shawl about her shoulders, and picked up her knitting from the floor where she had left it some hours before.

'Your father's in a lot of pain,' the doctor, an elderly, plump man from Brigg had told her, taking her by the arm. 'Not that he'd admit it. The thing is to keep him comfortable. It won't be long, now.'

Eleanor had known as much for some days. Her father had taken a turn for the worse. He needed constant nursing. The Rector's wife, Adelaide, and Betty Bowman, from the Sherwood Arms, had taken the School off her hands this last week. Simon Naismith-Parry and Group Captain Alexander had called on her, Adam visited the cottage most days, sat with her father for many hours, tried very hard to keep her spirits up but today the Lancasters had gone back to war and reclaimed him. Other than the doctor, there had been no visitors.

Last night Adam had waited until her father was asleep and crept down the stairs to join

Eleanor in the warm gloom before the fire.

'The Prof's dropped off, now,' he said quietly, lowering himself into the armchair. 'He's a little weaker today, I think.'

Eleanor had nodded.

'Absolutely on the ball, mind you,' Adam went on.

'I've asked the doctor to call again tomorrow.'

They had both seen the rapid decline in the old man. He was losing the struggle to conceal the pain. Eleanor's father was now confined to the big bed, unable to do the most basic of things for himself. He was helpless and hated it, all they could do was pretend not to notice and to try to maintain a semblance of normality around him. And carry on. Nothing mattered so much as to allow the old man to hold onto his pride.

'I think it is wise,' Adam had agreed.

'What did you talk about today?'

'This and that. Mostly shop. About Dave and Boscombe Down. We talked a lot about Boscombe Down. The Prof knew all the pilots on the Test Flight. The four of us who survived. The four musketeers, he used to call us.'

Eleanor had put down her book, marked her page.

Adam stared into the fire, his thoughts elsewhere.

'He asked me what had happened to the other two musketeers.'

'Max Reville and Bill Simmons?' Eleanor had prompted, the names were etched in her memory from reading and re-reading her brother's letters.

'Yes. Bill and Max.' Adam's voice was faraway.

Bill Simmons, the hearty sheep farmer from Auckland had died not far from where they now sat. It had happened in broad daylight in the middle of a blue, clear autumn sky. Two Spitfires had swooped out of the sun, swept down on the two Lancasters. The bombers had corkscrewed away into space: Adam's to port, Bill's to starboard. Adam had levelled N-Nan at five thousand feet over Messingham. Bill's aircraft, S-Sugar, had crashed into a field south of Yaddlethorpe. One of S-Sugar's rudders had snapped off. It was nobody's fault, just a harmless fighter affiliation evolution that went horribly wrong.

Max Reville, the indestructible flank forward who had won a Rugby Blue for Oxford before the war, was dead, too. He had been the passenger in the cab of a Bedford truck driven into the orbit of a Lancaster's idling starboard outer Merlin. His WAAF driver, recently arrived from 3 Group, had also been killed instantly. In those days 3 Group flew Stirlings and everybody knew you could drive a horse, cart and just about any kind of omnibus under a Stirling's wing with impunity. Max's WAAF driver had forgotten where she was and they had died for her trouble. These things happened.

'Both dead in accidents in England within a couple of weeks of each other. A month or so after Dave went missing on that Wismar show,' Adam reported, blankly.

Eleanor reached out, touched his hand.

'So, which musketeer were you?'

This broke Adam's reverie and returned him to the here and the now.

'Oh, that would be telling. But I think Dave

would certainly have been D'Artagnon.'

'The courageous, idealistic innocent abroad?'

'Something like that,' he nodded.

'I shall make a pot of tea,' Eleanor decided. 'If I leave you for a few minutes you won't go running away, will you?'

Adam had stayed until late. Very late. They had talked and talked. Although they remained physically apart they drew closer in every other way even if it was the intimacy of a brother and sister. In his mind he had marked out the boundaries, determined that whatever else he became he would never be her lover. Eleanor hated it in one way, yet loved him all the more in another. She knew that his was a world populated with ghosts; the ghosts of friends and countless brothers in arms. He thought he was doing the right thing; and that he was doing it for her. No matter how misplaced his fears he was doing it out of the purest of love, for her. On the doorstep at midnight they had embraced, and gently, a little tentatively, kissed.

'I do understand,' she had said. Although she knew he had known exactly what she meant Eleanor had spelled it out, anyway: 'But it is important to me,' she had explained, brazenly, 'that you know you don't have to be a perfect gentleman all the time, darling.'

'I know, but I think it's best this way...'

Eleanor sat in the rocking chair watching over her father, reflecting that without faith in the future one had nothing.

Her knitting needles clicked.

Chapter 14

Friday 17th December, 1943
RAF Waltham Grange, Lincolnshire

Shortly after the first Lancaster crashed a breath of wind briefly stirred the fog over the airfield and the flames of the burning bomber became, perversely, a beacon of hope. Suzy hovered at the back of the watchtower, listening as the controller and his WAAFs strived to avert total catastrophe. Their calmness belied the tragedy unfolding over Lincolnshire. Fog blanketed England from the Channel to the Scottish borders and the returning heavies were too low on fuel to divert to the fog-free fields of the West Country. The voices of the men in the Lancasters stacked over Waltham Grange filtered down to earth, disembodied, distorted by static.

"Hello Rabbit control. M-Mother. Over."

The prim, proper, studiously precise tones of the WAAF controllers replied, apparently untouched by the dreadfulness of the relentlessly unfolding disaster.

"Hello M-Mother, this is Rabbit control. Hold at three thousand, please."

"Hello Rabbit control. M-Mother. My engineer says we've got fifteen minutes fuel left. Repeat, fifteen minutes fuel left."

The duty controller leaned over the WAAF's shoulder, said something in her ear.

"Hello M-Mother, this is Rabbit control," she called. "Suggest you climb to five thousand. Vector zero-nine-zero. Repeat, climb to five thousand and abandon aircraft. Repeat, abandon aircraft."

"M-Mother to Rabbit control. Understood. Over."

"Good luck, M-Mother."

A gruff, Australian drawl came over the air.

"T-Tommy to Rabbit control. What's that glow on the ground?"

"Rabbit control to T-Tommy. The glow on the ground is a crashed aircraft approximately one quarter of a mile short of the flare path. Repeat, one quarter of a mile short of the flare path. Hold at two thousand feet."

More voices, quietly, politely clamoured for attention, salvation, hope in the fog.

"Hello Rabbit control. This is Q-Queenie. How much longer are we going to be stooging around up here…"

"R-Robert calling Rabbit control. Over…"

"Hello Rabbit control, P-Popsie…"

"Hello Rabbit control. F-Freddie. Over…"

One aircraft after another attempted to land, overshot or pulled up short of the runway, and climbed back up into the transient safety of the mists. Q-Queenie came in, missed the flare path, landed on the grassy infield, bumped harmlessly to a halt fifty yards from the watchtower surrounded by fire engines. Other bombers groped down through the fog, now and then finding sanctuary.

"Hello S-Sugar, this is Rabbit control. Call funnels. QFE one-oh-oh-seven…"

"Hello P-Popsie, this is Rabbit control. Pancake. Repeat, pancake!"

"Hello Z-Zebra, this is Rabbit control. Pancake!

Pancake!"

Flight-Lieutenant Ramsey touched Suzy's arm, quietly ushered her out of the watchtower.

"Nobody imagined it was going to be quite this bloody tonight," he said grimly as they stumbled through the mist in the direction of the Briefing Hall. "Not a word until we know for sure but they think the crashed kite is C-Charlie, the CO's kite."

"Oh."

"Poor old Hammy."

The tables were arranged at one end of the Briefing Hall. Three big trestle tables positioned several feet apart from each other. Although half-a-dozen Lancasters had got down so far, as yet none of their crews had arrived at the building. The Intelligence Officer paced behind the desks as if he was patrolling his own personal front line. His WAAF debriefers waited patiently. The Padre lurked in a corner. Suzy had never worked out exactly what purpose was served by the Padre's presence on these occasions. A large, clumsy trolley bearing a big hot water urn and piled high with mugs, bottles of milk, tins of sugar and biscuits had been wheeled over from the NAAFI.

Suzy settled beside the woman she had come to Waltham Grange to replace, Assistant Section Officer Margaret Warren. Maggie was older - by a year or two - than Suzy, frighteningly competent and knowledgeable, stoically determined to be cheerful, and positive at all times. She was married to an Australian, a 460 Squadron pilot, based at Binbrook. She was expecting a baby in April and was leaving both Waltham Grange and the RAF in a few days.

The two women had taken to each other immediately.

"The main thing is to be patient," Maggie had advised Suzy. "Listen to what the boys say, don't go hurrying them or putting words into their mouths. The Intelligence Officer, bless him, bombards the boys with questions, as if they've done something wrong, as if he's interrogating them. It doesn't work. The boys just clam up or worse, they start shooting lines. They do it deliberately, you know, just to rattle him. My advice is to let the boys give you the gen in their own time. A lot of them will talk their heads off if you give them a chance. I suppose they like to get it all off their chests."

The first crew trudged into the Hall.

"Maggie, my dear!" Hailed the pilot, heading directly towards the two women, ignoring the agitated gesturing of the Intelligence Officer who was pointing theatrically, at a table on the opposite side of the room. Margaret Warren smiled ruefully at the pilot as he unceremoniously dumped his kit on the floor and slumped onto the nearest chair. The rest of his crew began to make themselves at home. "Aren't you going to introduce me to your friend, Maggie?"

"This is Assistant Section Officer Mills, my replacement."

"Delighted, I'm sure."

"Suzy," Margaret said, glancing sidelong to her companion. "This is Squadron Leader Irving. The deputy CO."

"How do you do, sir," Suzy muttered, colouring with embarrassment. The display of unabashed familiarity shocked her more than somewhat.

"Welcome to Waltham Grange, my dear," Irving grinned, pausing to twirl the right handlebar of his magnificent ginger moustache. "What's this I hear about poor old Hammy, Maggie?"

The other members of his crew were eying Suzy with no little curiosity, apparently indifferent to the fate of their Squadron Commander.

"We think it is C in the field short of the flare path," Maggie replied, almost but not quite under her breath.

"Oh. Poor show."

"What's that?" Inquired the dapper, dark-haired Canadian at Irving's shoulder, lighting several cigarettes at once.

"It looks like Hammy's bought it, Don."

"Poor old Hammy..."

"Oh, bad show..."

"Looks like you're in charge now, Skipper."

Irving was handed a cigarette. He inhaled thoughtfully, exhaled with a sigh. Suzy guessed he was twenty-three or four and although he exuded assurance and bonhomie as if to the manner born, the abrupt realisation that he was now in command of 388 Squadron had, ever so briefly, knocked a little of the wind out of his sails.

"In that case we better get this over and done with, Maggie," he declared.

More crews trooped in and took their places in the queue. The trolley came around, dispensed tea, cocoa, biscuits and cigarettes while the story of the raid unfolded. Irving did most of the talking. He stuck to the plot, at pains to avoid embellishments.

"Some beggar dropped a line of fighter flares

right on top of us south of Groningen, almost hit one... The conditions were so bad I should imagine the Jerries only sent up their best men tonight... There were fighters working the route all the way from the coast to Hanover... Yes, I'd say we were up against chaps who knew their stuff, tonight... There were lots of combats... We counted at least a dozen kites going down..."

"Thirteen, I think, Skipper," corrected the dapper, dark-haired Canadian whom Suzy took to be Irving's navigator.

"Thirteen, then, Don."

"Yeah, thirteen," confirmed the Canadian, consulting his logs.

"What happened after Hanover?" Maggie asked, looking up from her notes.

"Things went a bit slack, actually," Irving remarked, in an assertively jovial tone which told the rest of his crew to shut up until spoken to. "Most of the fighters buggered off. Maybe, *they* sent them south because they thought we were off down to Leipzig, again. Either that or it was only the Deelen and St Trond boys who were able to get airborne, I daresay they'd have started running out of fuel after Hanover. Who knows? Things weren't too bad over the target. Plenty of cloud to blank out the searchlights and the flak wasn't up to its normal standard. Bit of an easy ride compared to the last few times we've been to the Big City."

"What about the marking?"

"No complaints. We found a nice big concentration of Sky Markers to bomb."

"Any big fires on the ground?"

"No. Not tonight."

"So, not much fighter activity over Berlin?"

"We saw a couple of combats on the way out. Otherwise, no sign of the beggars."

"Did you get an AP photo?"

"Yes. Probably just clouds, though…"

The dull, faraway sound of a large explosion came to their ears. The babble of voices in the Briefing Hall was momentarily stilled.

The windows rattled.

Squadron Leader Irving paused.

"Just clouds, don't you think, Dave?" He went on, literally not batting an eyelid as he turned to his bomb-aimer, a freckled boy.

"Clouds, Skipper," concurred the boy, cupping his cigarette in his left hand.

Suzy fought the coldness within. An icy, freezing hand clutched her heart. Another Lancaster had just crashed and yet the debriefing went on as if nothing had happened. Nothing at all.

"I'm off for a leak," declared one of Irving's gunners, the smallest, scruffiest member of the crew, rising and slouching out of the hall.

"No trouble on the way back," Irving reported. "Well, not until we got back home, anyway. The next time I bump into the Met Officer I'm going to give him a piece of my mind, I can tell you!"

Maggie asked more questions, prompting, probing for more information.

"Indications of jettisoning on the way out?" She asked softly, matter of factly. Out of the blue, without a hint of prejudice.

"No, not tonight," Irving told her, tersely. "Well, a couple of cookies half-way across the North Sea.

But those might have been kites turning back."

Presently, Irving's gunner returned.

"That was T that just crashed," he announced, matter of factly, resuming his seat. Suzy recalled T-Tommy's Australian pilot asking the controller about the glow on the ground short of the runway.

"Did anybody get out?"

"Nope."

Chapter 15

Friday 17th December, 1943
RAF Ansham Wolds, Lincolnshire

Over Lincolnshire the radio was a babble of voices, other pilots, crews, aircraft stacked over fog-bound fields waiting, hoping for a chance to land.

"Hello Chestnut control," Tilliard called through the static. "This is B-Beer. Over."

"Hello B-Beer, this is Chestnut control. Please hold at four thousand. Over."

Down in the broad valley of the River Trent the mist rolled down off the Lincolnshire Wold like a tsunami inundating the undulating fields below. Beneath B-Beer the fog eddied in pale, impenetrable, treacherous banks.

"Hello Chestnut control," Tilliard repeated, a little apologetically. "This is B-Beer, again. I have a casualty onboard."

"This is Chestnut control. Do you wish to declare an emergency, B-Beer?"

Tilliard thought hard about it. All he had to do was call out the magic word - *DARKIE* - and B-Beer would be advanced to the front of the queue.

"Negative, Chestnut control," he decided. "Over."

None of the others said a word. There was nothing to be said. There was no sign of Ansham Wolds's Sandra lights - the triangle of searchlights - set to cross above the aerodrome to welcome home 647 Squadron's heavies, nor sign of any other beacon.

The night fighter's cannon had stopped B-Beer's starboard outer Merlin, torn ragged lumps out of the wing and control surfaces, almost sent them to their doom forty miles north-east of Hanover. Only the extreme violence of Tilliard's evasive manoeuvres – both gunners reported a near collision with their attacker - and the cover of the clouds had enabled them to shake off the fighter.

Their hunter, a twin-engine Messerschmitt 110, had broken off the attack and decided to go in search of more quiescent, less energetic prey.

'If the wings come off, the wings come off,' an old lag once told him, early in his first tour on ops. 'That's the way it is. Nothing you can do about that. You can't afford to worry about it.'

Tonight he had very nearly ripped the wings off B-Beer. By rights they should be dead. Tilliard had recovered B-Beer from her headlong plunge at less than two thousand feet. The engineer had shouted a warning that the starboard outer was smoking, he had feathered the engine, activated the fire extinguisher and prayed. Miraculously, the fire had gone out. After that they had climbed as high as the crippled bomber would climb - six thousand feet - jettisoned their bombs, limped home by the most direct route, threading their way past and around known trouble spots. Ironically, the clouds which had shielded them from the hunters over Germany, might well be the death of them, now.

If it was going to happen tonight, so be it.

Tilliard was trembling with exhaustion and B-Beer was flying like she was looking for an excuse to fall out of the sky. Any excuse. A moment's carelessness, a moment's inattention and she would kill them. Notwithstanding, he was not about to jump the landing queue. They would take their turn. Take their chances. Nobody jumped the queue on a night like this. That was the way the game was played. The laws might be unwritten but they were understood by all.

"Jack, can you still hear me?" Tilliard asked, coaxing the Lancaster into a gentle, wide circuit over Lincolnshire.

"Loud and clear, Skipper!"

"How's Tom?"

Jack Gordon had still been in the astrodome when Tilliard had thrown B-Beer into the first right-hand corkscrew. Centrifugal force had lifted the navigator off his feet, smashed him into the canopy above his head, then dumped him back on the floor. Dazed, disorientated he had groped for a handhold, anticipating the next stomach-wrenching manoeuvre. When it came he was hurled head first into the unyielding, cold steel of the armoured back panel of the pilot's seat and he had not regained consciousness until some minutes later. By then the excitement was over. Bloodied and shaken he had immediately declared himself to be 'in one piece' and got on with things. Not so poor Tom Dennison. Jack now crouched over the prostrate, unmoving form of B-Beer's W/T operator in the waist of the Lancaster. He flicked his intercom switch.

"The same, Skipper."

Cannon fire had smashed through the floor of the fuselage, demolished the vacant navigator's position, wrecked the *H2S* and *Gee* sets, scorched and shredded Jack's maps and charts, and scattered the shattered remnants of his escape kit throughout the mid-section of the fuselage. Something, either a lump of shrapnel or perhaps even an unexploded cannon shell had caught Tom Dennison in the midriff and judging by the amount of blood he had lost, very nearly cut him in half. The boy's blood glinted evilly in the beam of Jack's torch. With Billy Campbell's help, he had lifted Dennison over the main spar, laid him on the floor, attempted to examine the extent of his wounds and applied dressings to the ones he could see. Watching Jack working on the W/T operator, the bomb-aimer, had at one point, fainted.

Jack had slapped him, shaken him.

'Stay with him, Billy.'

'What do I do it he comes round?'

'You hold his hand and you keep him still. If he's in pain you give him a shot of morphine! I've got to figure out where we are and work out a heading for home. I'll be back as soon as I can. Stay with him. Are you okay?'

'I'm okay,' the boy had nodded.

Jack had scrabbled through the wreckage, blood and worse, searching for any logs and any charts which had survived.

The flight engineer, an unflappable Rhodesian who had come to Bomber Command via a cattle farm outside Bulawayo, had tapped him on the shoulder, shouted in his ear above the roar of the slipstream whistling through countless jagged holes in the fuselage.

'The Skipper wants to know the score back there, Jack?'

'I think Tom's still breathing, but I can't be

sure. He's bleeding bad.'

The engineer had leaned close. 'What about you? You don't look so good yourself?'

Jack had shrugged.

'I'm fine. Tell the Skipper it looks like the W/T's in one piece and that I've found enough of my kit to do some dead reckoning. With a bit of luck we should be able to get close enough to home to pick up the base beam.'

That was over four hours ago.

"Jack," Tilliard said, breaking into the navigator's thoughts. "See if you can get a static line attached to Tom."

"Roger, Skipper." Just when you thought things could not get any worse, they did. That was ops for you!

"Pilot to crew. It looks as if we're going to be stooging around hereabouts for a while. None of the dials are reading empty, yet. I'll let you know when they do. Anybody who wants to can bale out then. Jack, if it comes to it, will you look after Tom?"

"Roger, Skipper."

Tom Dennison groaned, stirred. The W/T operator's eyes opened, briefly.

"Don't try to move, Tom," Jack told him.

The wounded man's face contorted with pain.

"What..."

"We got jumped by a fighter. You've been out for the count but we're back over England. We're in the stack. Over the airfield. We're nearly home. You'll be in hospital in no time."

Dennison stared up into the navigator's face in the gloom.

"Christ, you look frigging awful, Jack," he forced out, wincing horribly with every breath.

"So do you, you miserable beggar!"

Jack fumbled in the first aid kit. His fingers closed around a morphine ampoule. His mind was made up. He would not bale out. Not now he knew Tom was alive. Even if he could get the W/T operator to the door, the jump would kill the boy. Besides, if Peter Tilliard thought his chum Jack Gordon was going to leave him to his own devices in the fog he had another frigging thing coming!

He flicked his intercom switch.

"Skipper, Tom's just come round."

"Good. Take care of him, Jack. We'll get down somehow."

As Jack injected the morphine into Dennison's arm he was oddly at peace with himself, strangely unafraid. It was fate. Nothing personal, just fate. If he lived until the morning it meant he was destined to marry Nancy Bowman, raise a brood of well-fed, mischievous children, find himself a country pub to run after the war and to live happily ever more.

Tom Dennison's gaze went glassy and he passed out.

Chapter 16

Friday 17th December, 1943
RAF Waltham Grange, Lincolnshire

At noon Squadron Leader Clive Irving, the acting CO of 388 Squadron, walked into the Operations Room. He slumped into a chair in front of the readiness board, put his feet on the table and glanced across to the Operations Officer, Flight-Lieutenant Ramsey.

"Okay, old son," he sighed, wearily, fishing out a pack of cigarettes from his tunic pocket. "Tell me the worst!"

Ramsey pushed two typewritten sheets under his nose.

"Command put up four hundred and eighty odd Lancs last night, sir. A new record. Twenty-five are missing, about five percent of the force. Not as bad as we thought, given the fighter activity on the outward leg. However, at least thirty Lancs crashed or ditched in the sea. The fog seems to have been worst over our fields and those of the Pathfinders, Five Group got off relatively lightly."

Suzy had been standing outside the door of the office when Irving made his entrance.

'Clive Irving was Harry's, my husband's, best man at our wedding,' Maggie Warren had explained, confidentially, earlier that morning when the last of the crews had been debriefed. 'They were both with Wing-Commander Chantrey at Kelmington last year. That's where I met Harry. Anyway, it was about this time last year that Harry got himself smashed up in a car crash, he's only just got back onto ops. Clive turned up here out of the blue in July, a couple of weeks after Wing-Commander Chantrey took over. Between you and me, I think there was a bit of poaching involved.'

"Bit of a black, what!" Irving snorted, pushing the sheets of paper away. "Still, worse things happen at sea! Isn't that what they say?"

"I believe so, sir."

Out on the airfield they were recovering the bodies from the charred wrecks of C-Charlie and T-Tommy. Several aircraft from other squadrons which had found safe haven at Waltham Grange were being checked over and readied to fly back to their home fields. Other Lancasters were being inspected, overhauled. No matter what calamity befell the Main Force the routine of the stations continued unchanged, immutable. Last night's battle was over, it was history; the most important battle was always the next one.

"What's the forecast for tomorrow?"

"More fog, sir."

"Oh, joy!"

"Then clearer at the start of next week."

Irving jumped to his feet.

"Any more news of our lost sheep?"

Four of 388 Squadron's Lancasters had landed away.

"They should all be back by this evening, sir."

"That's something." Irving stalked out.

Suzy was flagging. She had not slept that night, worked non-stop. There were reams of debriefing notes to collate, summaries to be prepared, reports to fill in, check, and double check. The paperwork generated by a major operation was awesome and the voluminous red tape mind-numbingly convoluted.

Despite her weariness she could not help but worry about Peter. Had he been flying last night? Was he safe? They had not seen each other for nearly seven weeks and she had no idea when they would see each other again.

"There's a call in the Flight Office for Assistant Section Officer Mills."

Suzy blinked, her tiredness evaporating.

"A call?"

A hundred horrible, dark thoughts jangled in her head.

"A telephone call, ma'am," she was told, patiently.

Suzy stumbled into the corridor, hurried the short distance to the Flight Office.

"There's supposed to be a call for me?"

"Over there."

The receiver lay on the desk top. Suzy stood over the receiver for a moment, gathered herself. Very slowly, tentatively, she reached out for it and lifted it to her ear.

"Hello," she said, with a bravura that she hardly felt.

"Suzy, is that you?"

"Peter!" She cried out. Every head in the room turned in her direction: she did not care. Peter Tilliard was alive, well and at the other end of the line. She unashamedly surrendered her normal reserve, forgot for a moment her dignity. "Peter, darling!"

It was a bad line, it clicked and echoed.

"Suzy! How are you, darling?"

"I'm fine, silly. How are you? Were you flying last night? I was so worried, what with all that ghastly fog?"

The man did not reply immediately. He hesitated and the woman read volumes into his hesitation.

"I'm fine. Fine..."

"I've missed you terribly, darling."

"And I've missed..."

The line clicked loudly and went dead. Suzy groaned out aloud in frustration.

"Everything okay?" Maggie asked as Suzy emerged from the Flight Office, her face a picture of concern.

"We got cut off."

"Oh. It wasn't bad news, then?"

"Goodness, no!" Suzy smiled, brightly. She had not confided in the other woman about Peter. In fact, she had told very few people about Peter; her parents a week ago, one or two of the girls on her course at Shrewsbury, otherwise she had kept him as her secret, locked in her heart.

"I guessed that you probably had somebody flying last night, that's all," Maggie said, sympathetically.

"Was it that obvious?"

"Only to me. Let's go and get a cup of tea," suggested the older woman. "You can tell me all about him."

Chapter 17

Friday 17th December, 1943
The Gatekeeper's Lodge, Ansham Wolds, Lincolnshire

Eleanor had expected him. She had known he would come, even if it was for no more than a brief visit. Adam Chantrey was a creature of habit. At first, she had not understood this, realising only belatedly that he was a man who drew strength from routine, and craved orderliness amidst the madness.

Recognising his knock at the door she skipped down the stairs to let him in. He always knocked firmly. Three knocks, loud enough to carry through the cottage but not so loudly as to give anybody inside a start.

"And how's the Prof today?" Adam inquired, smiling. The wintery gloom of the early evening could not hide the strain, nor his lack of sleep.

"Bearing up."

Eleanor shut the door, locking out the damp, cold fog. That afternoon the Rector had called, face like death.

"Everything's all right," Simon Naismith-Parry had said, breathlessly quickly, so as to deny her fears the opportunity to multiply. "Your young man is perfectly all right. As soon as I heard I had to come to see you before you got wind of the wild rumours flying around the village."

Something awful had happened in the fog.

'There was another big raid on Berlin last night.

According to the BBC twenty-five aircraft are missing, but that's not the half of it. People are saying dozens of Lancasters have crashed. I popped into the Sherwood Arms on the way over and spoke to Arnold Bowman, he usually knows what's going on. He told me 647 Squadron lost four aircraft last night, and it was just about the same everywhere in One Group. Goodness knows how many aircraft have been lost. But the main thing is that Adam is all right.'

Eleanor had not had the heart to tell Simon that two days ago Adam had mentioned to her, casually but in no way idly, that he was about to send Ben Hardiman and the rest of his crew on leave. Pointedly, he had remarked that 'these days I never fly ops with strangers'. She looked into Adam's eyes. "It must have been horrible last night," she offered, pursing her lips.

"No, not so good," he admitted with a shrug. "So it goes. I'm afraid I don't have long. Sorry."

Eleanor planted a kiss on his cheek.

"It's lovely to see you, even if it's not for long."

"There's a big bash in the Mess tonight," he explained, lamely. "It would be bad form to miss it. My presence, is, er, expected. As it were."

Eleanor was amazed how swiftly she had become accustomed to the ways of Bomber Command. The Squadron had had a bad night; it had happened before, it would happen again. Probably sooner rather than later. Tonight the crews were throwing a party, a wake in honour of the fallen. Like gladiators who had survived mortal combat in the arena they were celebrating, in the certain knowledge that their turn might come tomorrow.

"Go up and see father," she suggested. "I shall put the kettle on."

The Prof was propped up in the big bed.

"Ah, the warrior returns," he sighed, forcing his thin, pale lips into a half-smile. The dry, grey flesh was drawn slackly over his cheek bones. His eyes were sunken. Despite his debilitation the old man still had his wits about him and he made a particular point of demonstrating as much whenever a visitor called. In between he collapsed into helplessness, and let Eleanor nurse him how ever she wished. "So, how goes the war in Sparta?"

Adam chuckled, settled himself in the rocking chair.

"Not so well, Prof."

"How so?" Adam viewed him thoughtfully. Ever since the old man's arrival in Ansham Wolds, they had discussed service and operational matters with a frankness that hitherto, would have been unthinkable.

"Something like an eighth of the Lancaster Force went for a burton last night."

The old man's eyes widened. "Fifty or sixty Lancs?"

"Nearer sixty so far as I can tell," Adam confided. "Bloody fog. Over thirty kites crashed in England. We think the raid was successful. Fairly successful, anyway. We're going to need the Halifaxes in tow if we're going to crack Berlin, of course."

Eleanor's father coughed a painful, racking cough, struggled to catch his breath. Presently, he recovered. Nodded, sagely.

"Their incendiary loads make a big difference," he agreed. As the devastation on the ground spread, the key thing was to scatter the largest possible number of incendiaries. High explosives shattered and splintered, only fire consumed. The Halifaxes, with their all-incendiary cargoes would be sorely missed if the Chief left the fight to the Lancaster Force alone. "How fared Ansham Wolds last night?"

"Middling to awful," Adam confessed, without ado. "Mustn't complain, though. I gather the Pathfinders at Warboys lost seven kites in the fog."

"Ninety-Seven Squadron," recalled the Prof. The effort drained him. "Ninety-Seven Squadron are at Warboys, aren't they?"

"Yes." Adam lapsed into silence, aware that conversation sapped the old man's strength; that words were precious and not to be wasted, misspent exploring cul-de-sacs. It was very dark in the room. He rose from the rocking chair and lit the candle on the bedside table. The Prof's cold, bony hand reached out, grasped the younger man's wrist and the old man's tired, rheumy eyes held him for a moment.

"Why on earth haven't you asked Eleanor to marry you?"

"Because it wouldn't be fair on her." He replied, truthfully.

"Oh, fairness, is it?"

"What with things being the way they are."

"Ha!" Croaked the old man, his voice trailing away. "It goes without saying you'd have my blessing. Things being what they are, or not! There, I've said it. I shall say no more on the subject."

Eleanor was waiting for Adam in the parlour. He joined her by the fire, watched her pour the tea.

"No Johnny or Emmy?"

"At the Bowman's," she smiled. "Probably picking up lots of bad habits from the Bowman's evacuees."

"Don't you mind?"

"Gracious, no! They won't always live in sleepy old Ansham. One day they'll have to go out into the big wide world and then they'll need all the bad habits they can get if they're going to survive."

Adam laughed gently, said nothing.

"If they're going to survive, and prosper, anyway," Eleanor added, ruefully. "And I do want them to prosper. If at all possible."

"So you should."

"You're going to be late for your bash, darling."

"Yes, I ought to be heading back," he apologised.

They held hands in the doorway.

"Off you go," Eleanor chided him.

She watched him trudge to the Bentley, drop behind the wheel and fire up the engine. He waved and was gone, gunning the motor in the night. Eleanor stared into the darkness. He dreamed of fire and of death on the roads to high Germany. She dreamed another dream. In her dream there were no flames, and the killing was over. In her dream they were together as man and wife, and they and their children prospered in the peace she believed, with all her heart, would come one day.

One day.

Chapter 18

Friday 17th December, 1943
RAF Ansham Wolds, Lincolnshire

"Well?" Asked Jack Gordon.

"Well what?" Tilliard retorted, slamming the door and tossing his cap onto his cot.

"Did you get through to Waltham Grange, you clot?"

"Yes."

"And?"

"Suzy's fine!" Tilliard sat down, surveyed his friend's bruised, swollen countenance. "It took me ages to get through, and then no sooner than we get talking the bloody line goes down!"

"But she's okay?" Jack persisted.

"Yes, Suzy's fine."

"And she knows you're fine, too?"

Tilliard nodded, viewing Jack ruefully. His navigator ought by rights to be in hospital. His left arm was in a sling, protecting a cracked collar bone. His right cheek was gashed, stitched and swollen. Beneath his battledress his spare, sinewy frame was a mass of cuts and bone deep bruises, mottled black and blue.

'Look, he should be kept in for observation, at the very least!' The Flight Surgeon had protested.

'Sorry, Doc. No can do!' Tilliard had declared. 'Jack's got an appointment in Kingston Magna and he's jolly well going to keep it. And that's that! I'll bring him back afterwards. Then you can do whatever you like with him.'

Jack was not a pretty sight.

"Are you sure this is a good idea?" The Australian protested, feebly. "We could do it tomorrow."

"We're doing it today, Jack!"

"I can hardly bloody walk!"

"I'll carry you if I have to!"

It was mid-afternoon by the time they finally set off. Peter Tilliard drove through the gates of the station, pointed the car down the hill towards Kingston Magna. Wreaths of mist were forming over the fields as the premature winter dusk descended. The conditions were eerily reminiscent of the previous afternoon and sent an involuntary shiver down his spine.

Most of the gauges had been reading EMPTY when B-Beer's wheels finally touched the ground. Nobody had elected to bale out but at the first engine misfire Tilliard would have ordered everybody out, anyway. In the event the Lancaster had probably been flying on fumes for several minutes when he saw a flare through a break in the cloud, steered for it and a few seconds later glimpsed the Sandra lights dimly coned above the airfield. Groping into the murk, sliding down to earth blindly, despairingly, the flare path had magically materialised beneath them and a little to port. A kick on the rudder bar, one last burst of revs on the three good throttles and B-Beer had lined up. Brilliant white flames from the oil-burning goose-neck flares marked out the runway, and drums of burning petrol, hastily arranged in a chevron at the threshold warned the unwary not to put down too soon.

The Lancaster sank down onto the cold, damp tarmac. Tyres kissed the runway, squealed, adhered to terra firma and the bomber ran headlong into a thick bank of mist. Tilliard had held the aircraft steady, prayed a quick prayer. After an eternity B-Beer had hurtled into clearer air and he had gingerly applied the brakes.

Nothing had happened.

"No pressure, Skipper!"

"Hang on everybody!" Tilliard had yelled.

He had allowed B-Beer to drift off the runway, bump and jolt onto the infield, chopped back on the throttles, yelled at the engineer to cut all the switches and with a silent prayer, let the bomber run straight into the darkness, across the grass. The Lancaster had eventually rumbled to a halt a hundred yards short of the bomb dump...

Jack Gordon nursed his aches and pains in the passenger seat as Tilliard cautiously negotiated the narrow lanes. For once the rambunctious Australian was silent, somewhat lost in his thoughts. His friend drove the Austin like an old woman, mechanically, nervously as if he had absolutely no feel for the vehicle. Fortunately, he handled a Lancaster with considerably more élan. That was the only reason they were all still alive and the reason why nobody had opted to bale out when the Skipper reported the gauges were reading EMPTY.

"You're very quiet, Jack?"

"Contemplating my fate, that's all."

"So you should be!"

Tilliard grimaced. His good humour was forced. Every time he closed his eyes he was confronted by the horrific sight that had greeted him in the midsection of the Lancaster after they had rolled to a standstill. Picking his way through the wreckage he had come upon Jack and the unconscious W/T Operator. Jack was covered in Tom Dennison's blood. It was on his hands, on his arms up to his elbows, on his face, in his lap.

Absolutely everywhere.

"If Gordon hadn't staunched the worst of the bleeding young Dennison would have bled to death," the Flight Surgeon had declared. "As it is, he's got a fighting chance." A fighting chance. Either way, Tom's tour was finished. If he survived the night, tomorrow he would be transferred to a hospital in Hull.

Since Jack was going to be out of commission for at least a week or two, Tilliard had sent the rest of the crew off on leave. There was no profit in having the chaps moping around the aerodrome thinking about Tom.

Last night the Luftwaffe and the fog had inflicted an unprecedented catastrophe upon the Lancaster Force. Command had confirmed that 59 Lancasters had been lost. Of these aircraft, two - from Elsham Wolds had crashed shortly after the off - and 32 had crashed in the fog on their return from Germany. The crews were already calling it 'Black Thursday'.

647 Squadron was also counting the cost. Of the 22 Lancasters it had despatched two A Flight aircraft, L-Lincoln and T-Tommy were missing, and one B and one C Flight aircraft had crashed. Both had been in the hands of sprogs: O-Orange with a crew on its third op, N-Nan's on its second. O-

Orange had flown into the rising ground east of the station, killing every man onboard. N-Nan had crash-landed and caught fire at Bardney. Miraculously, only two of her crew were dead.

It had been so good to hear Suzy's voice again after so many weeks of silence...

Six kites gone already this month: in only three ops.

No. No, this was the wrong time to brood over spilt milk.

This was a time to think of something else; of Suzy, or Jack's forthcoming confrontation with the father of the bride to be, or of the long overdue furlough the Wingco wanted him to take, anything but last night. Anything but the fresh arterial blood soaking into Jack's sheepskins and washing about on the floor of the kite...

Tilliard parked the car in the lane in front of the *Hare and Hounds* and turned to his friend.

"In the circumstances, I won't ask if you're feeling fit, Jack."

"Very funny!"

"No second thoughts?"

Jack smiled crookedly, painfully.

"Not on your life, mate!"

Chapter 19

Friday 17th December, 1943
RAF Ansham Wolds, Lincolnshire

Peter Tilliard viewed the Wingco's big black wolf, Rufus, lapping contentedly at the mugs of stout the Station Master and the Adjutant had put down for him by the bar. Rufus slurped loudly, greedily at one, then the next as he worked his way down the line.

"I don't know how the old fellow does it, sir," Tilliard remarked, chuckling. "A couple of pints and I'm out for the count."

"Practice makes perfect, Peter," Adam Chantrey grinned. The Wingco was looking tired, as if he badly needed a night or two of uninterrupted sleep. The wake was gathering momentum around them but Tilliard could tell the CO's heart was not in it. It was not an obvious thing, it took an old lag to know it. "What have you done with Jack Gordon, Peter? I saw you two skulking off earlier! It's not like Jack to miss a do like this?"

The Mess was filling up. The smell of tobacco smoke, beer, sweat and wet overcoats was pronounced. The Mess always smelled of wet overcoats, even when it was dry outside. Without the smell of damp serge, the Mess simply would not be the Mess.

"No, sir," Tilliard laughed, determined to jolly his CO along and jog him into the spirit of the occasion. In this business a fellow was entitled to a melancholy day now and then. You owed it to a man to pretend nothing was amiss. Especially, when you recognised he had had a bellyful of ops. "When you saw us earlier we were off on a rather dicey op, actually, sir."

"Oh?" The Wingco returned, intrigued, brightening as he sipped his beer.

There was a minor commotion in the middle of the room; one or two of the chaps were clearing away tables and chairs to make a space to dance in. Tonight, the idea was that the 'event' would kick off in the Mess and later progress to the gymnasium, where the station band would play for a 'proper' dance. That at least, was the idea.

"Jack didn't make it back to base, I'm afraid."

"Oh, dear. Poor show."

"I think he's landed on his feet, though!" Tilliard laughed. "More by luck than design, mind you."

"Ah, I see. Who's the lucky girl?"

"Nancy Bowman. Bill Bowman' youngest," Tilliard explained, barely able to contain his mirth. "Not to say fairest."

"Bowman?"

"He has the *Hare and Hounds* in Kingston Magna."

"The *Hare and Hounds*?"

"Best watering hole for miles around."

"I'll have to take you word for it, Peter." Chantrey slapped his shoulder, shook his head. There was a mischievous twinkle in his eye, again. He had, for the moment at least, put aside his demons. "Nancy Bowman must be quite a girl. Getting a fellow like Jack Gordon down the aisle."

Tilliard nodded, recollecting the afternoon's

work.

'Hello, Jack. Mister Tilliard.' *Iron-fisted* Bill Bowman had grunted, flatly. His ruddy face bore its usual amiable expression but his eyes had been hard, flinty grey and suspicious. He had focussed on Jack Gordon's bruised face. 'You'll be wanting to talk to me in the back room, I'm thinking.'

'If we might, Bill,' Tilliard had suggested.

They had followed Nancy's father into the snug.

'My word, you look a sight for sore eyes, Jack,' Bill Bowman had commented, quietly shutting the door at their backs.

'Bit of bother with a fighter,' the Australian had muttered, the words slurring from his swollen lips. 'I'm okay. It looks a lot worse than it is. Poor Tom Dennison caught a packet. He's not so good.'

'I'm sorry to hear that. He's a good lad.'

Tilliard had coughed, decided to take the initiative.

'Bill, Jack's got something to ask you. Haven't you, Jack?'

'Er, yes.'

'I'm waiting,' Bill Bowman assured the younger men, not without a certain menace.

'It's about Nancy,' Jack began, painfully straightening to his full height, standing as tall as his cracked ribs permitted. If he was going to take a punch he was going to take it like a man, not cringing like a beaten dog. He met the older man's eye, unflinchingly. 'I'm crazy about her. And that's the truth, Bill. I have been since the first time I set eyes on her and I want to marry her!'

Tilliard had anticipated having to badger and cajole Jack into doing the right thing, but Jack had come up trumps. He was proud of him. The funny thing was he got the distinct impression that nobody was more stunned than Jack Gordon himself.

'With your permission, of course, Bill?'

All the tension had ebbed out of the broad, ox-like frame of the landlord of the *Hare and Hounds*. Suddenly, he was smiling the smile of a man whose belief in the fundamental goodness of human nature had just been restored. Shortly afterwards, Tilliard had left Jack in the tender loving care of his bride to be. Nancy and her mother had taken instant pity on the wounded hero, insisted on personally nursing him back to rude health. He had beaten a hasty retreat, leaving Jack to his fate. He recounted the scene, unabridged, for his CO's entertainment.

"My word, Jack's face must have been a picture!"

Suddenly there was pandemonium.

"Make way!"

"Mind your backs, chaps!"

"Look lively, there!"

The loudest call was unmistakably, that of Henry Barlow, B Flight's oldest lag. Oddly, another shouted warning came from the lips of the Padre, the Reverend Poore.

"Mind out there! 'B' Flight cycle section coming!"

"AND THEY'RE OFF!" Yelled the Padre, his voice cracking.

Bodies scattered in all directions. Bicycles ridden by frantically pedalling airmen burst into the crowded Mess. In a moment the wake was reduced to utter bedlam. Half the gathering cheered, the rest jeered, clapped, shook fists. Adam stepped back out of the melee, levered himself onto the bar where he sat, smiling broadly, surveying the chaos with undiluted satisfaction. The leading bicycle never made the first turn around the big iron stove. It clattered into a chair, skidded, tipped its rider headlong. The next bike piled into the first, depositing the burly frame of Henry Barlow on top of the fallen man. Other bicycles clattered by. Slowly, carefully the downed jockeys disentangled themselves. The two men exchanged a look, collapsed in laughter. Stomach-wrenching, uncontrollable laughter.

The crowd closed around them.

Adam noted the Padre standing by the door, arms crossed, aloof from the mayhem, smiling. Jumping down from his vantage point on the bar top, he pushed through the throng, and threw his arms around the two fallen racers as they gingerly picked themselves up from the floor.

"That was a bloody awful landing, Henry!" He declared to the South African. Then he turned, fixed his stare on the perspiring, breathless face of his opponent. "Welcome to 647 Squadron, Bob."

Squadron Leader Nicholson dusted himself off, grinned lopsidedly, and very self-consciously.

"Thank you, sir. I'm jolly glad to be here."

Unseen, the Reverend Poore made his exit, headed for the station gymnasium to oversee the final arrangements for the dance.

Chapter 20

Monday 20th December, 1943
RAF Ansham Wolds, Lincolnshire

The Main Force was on for Frankfurt-am-Main. Christmas was coming but not for the cities on the plain. Tonight, the aiming point was in the *Altstadt* and the Halifaxes were rejoining the battle and sharing the pain.

Three days after 'Black Thursday', Bomber Command was laying its newest ghosts to rest and going back to war. The Met Officer promised that visibility over the target would be 'excellent' and accordingly, the Pathfinders were reverting to the old, tried and tested ground marking drill. Frankfurt's fate it seemed was sealed.

Adam was unconvinced; today was one of those days when he simply did not completely have his heart in his work. At the main crew briefing he sat and awaited his turn, his face a mask. His crews had breathed easier discovering Frankfurt was the target. Anywhere was better than the Big City.

The crews took it for granted that the aiming point would be in the *Altstadt* because that was where the kindling was best. The Intelligence Officer also informed them that Frankfurt was the largest city in Hessen, the headquarters of the *IG Farben-Industrie* chemicals combine and a key communications and transportation centre. He neglected to tell them that Frankfurt was the birthplace of Goethe and the ancient capital of the Eastern Frankish kingdom, from whence the city's name descended. Nor did he tell them that since the middle ages Frankfurt had been one of the great trading centres of Europe, famous for its fairs. Not that it mattered. The crews hardly listened to his spiel. Sadly, understandably, they did not care about the history of the city. Goethe, chemical works, and legends of Frankish kings meant nothing to them. They were rather more preoccupied with the night fighters, the guns and the searchlights defending the *target*, and far too busy fretting in case there was fog over their fields when they got back. If they got back. The Intelligence Officer droned on, interminably.

Eventually, Adam coughed loudly, scowled darkly.

He was losing count of the number of times he had reminded the bloody man to keep things short, sweet and to the point on these occasions. It was not that the man was a fool, or even that he unduly liked the sound of his own voice. In fact he was a former teacher of English, a decent, decidedly earnest man of indeterminate middle years, with a remarkable grasp for detail. The problem was he talked to the crews as if they were schoolboys cramming for an open entrance exam.

'Tell the chaps what they're bombing,' was the terse diktat. 'Why it's important. Why it matters. Then tell them the latest gen about hot spots along the route. Then get off the blasted stage!'

Evidently, the well-meaning, scholarly Intelligence Officer still had not got the message. Adam made a mental note to the effect that his next 'pep talk' with the man would neither be overlong, nor overly cordial.

"Er, right chaps," announced the Intelligence Officer, belatedly catching his CO's eye. "That's all I've got to say. I shall pass you back to the senior briefing officer."

Bob Nicholson jumped up. It was his first experience of orchestrating a main crew briefing at Ansham Wolds. He was nervous and his nervousness accentuated the nasal quality of his raised voice.

Later, much later when Ansham Wolds's heavies were half-way to Frankfurt, Adam found his second-in-command leafing through technical manuals in B Flight's claustrophobic, cluttered office at the back of the hangars.

"Only the one early return so far," he commented, waving Nicholson to stay where he was. Nobody stood on ceremony when the crews were in the air. Not on his Squadron.

"You can rely on me to have stiff words in the morning, sir," promised the other man. The early returner was B-Beer, a new aircraft of that designation replacing the badly damaged bomber – subsequently written off and currently being salvaged for spare parts – that Peter Tilliard had brought back from Berlin, flown by one of B Flight's most experienced pilots. The aircraft's rear turret had malfunctioned, some sort of hydraulic failure. Assuming the fault was genuine, this qualified as a perfectly honourable reason to abort an operation before reaching the enemy coast. Nicholson was studying the relevant hydraulic and electrical diagrams. He was taking the early return very, very personally. "The maintenance chief is checking the turret, now, sir."

"Oh," Adam sighed. "I see."

It was his practice to leave his Flight Commanders to their own devices, let them get on with it unless they made a complete hash of things. He expected his Flight Commanders to train their crews until they dropped, or at least until they attained a respectable level of operational competence, and thereafter to make sure, damned sure, that they pressed on, more or less regardless. It was easier for Mac and Peter to drive their crews on because they were respected old lags, able to lead from the front; Nicholson remained unblooded on Lancasters. Until he got a few ops under his belt he was in an invidious position and there was little Adam could do to help him. Bob was going to have to earn the respect of his crews the hard way, by dint of his own actions.

"Mind if I park myself in here for a bit?" Adam asked.

"No, of course not, sir."

Adam lit a cigarette. He and his second-in-command would never be friends. Nor would they ever communicate on wavelengths as closely attuned as those he shared with Mac or Peter Tilliard. In itself, this was unimportant. What mattered was that they sang from the same songbook. Whether they liked each other was incidental, whether they presented a united front to the crews was everything.

"I hear you've recruited a crew, Bob?"

"Yes. Sound fellows."

Adam took this as a sign he did not want to discuss the subject. There had been no rush of volunteers to fly with Nicholson, consequently, he had gathered a motley collection of sprogs and spare men straight from the Group depot. Nicholson was too long away from the squadrons to be able to bring in men with whom he had previously flown ops. A year away was an awfully long time on ops.

"You'll be back on ops soon enough, Bob."

"I jolly well hope so, sir!"

Adam shrugged, smoked his cigarette.

Things would be simpler if Nicholson had been more prepared to accept a helping hand when he first arrived at Ansham Wolds. Adam blamed himself. He had allowed his personal reservations to cloud his judgement. He should have taken a stronger line from the outset, given his second-in-command the support – muscular support if necessary - and encouragement he had every right to expect from his new CO. Specifically, he ought to have ordered, rather than suggested that Peter Tilliard take the man under his wing from day one.

"I've been trying to get back on ops for the last six months," Nicholson went on. "I'm not a great one for sitting around."

Adam put his feet up on a convenient stool, dozed. Nobody could be on the ball every minute of every day, it paid to snatch forty winks when you could, let your guard down every now and then.

Bob Nicholson had not learned that yet.

If he did not learn it quickly it would kill him in a hurry.

Chapter 21

Wednesday 22nd December, 1943
Lancaster F-Freddie, 5 miles West of Gainsborough, Lincolnshire

From 15,000 feet the River Trent, the great storm drain of the East Midlands and Lincolnshire was a muddy, grey ribbon meandering north up to Gainsborough. The cloud was broken and the winter sun bright, dazzling in the cockpit. Peter Tilliard basked in the warmth of the light, braced behind the armoured back of the pilot's seat. The Lancaster had been in the air over two hours, criss-crossing the Pennines, paying two visits to the bombing range at Upton St. Thomas, dropping live thousand pounders on both occasions. Several times during the flight he had suddenly bawled at the pilot to take evasive action.

'FIGHTER ATTACKING! CORKSCREW PORT! GO! GO! GO!'

Squadron Leader Bob Nicholson had responded with great gusto, thrown the aircraft about with increasing abandon and a burgeoning confidence.

'Don't hold back, old man,' Tilliard had coached him. 'Don't hesitate. Take it from me these kites will take an awful lot of stick!'

Nicholson was an accomplished pilot but he was ring rusty and accustomed to the gentler, less responsive characteristics of his beloved, lumbering Stirlings. The raw power and proven robustness of the Lanc had come as something of a rude shock.

'When in doubt, push the throttles through the

gate and let your Merlins get you out of trouble,' he had drilled into his pupil and now, at last, B Flight's commander was making real progress. Today's exercise was the culmination of a short, brutal introduction to Lancasters: Bob Nicholson's 'corkscrew run'. Today's exercise would expose any remaining weakness, any lack of proficiency. Unknown to Nicholson, if he and his crew passed this test, they would be cleared to fly ops.

'Peter,' the Wingco asked, taking Tilliard aside the previous day. 'How close to ops is Bob?'

'Close, sir. He's getting the hang of things.'

"Good. Push him hard, Peter. If he's ready for the corkscrew run, put him through it tomorrow."

Tilliard read volumes into the Wingco's sudden urgency. The CO knew he was about to be screened. Sooner rather than later Bob was going to be left holding the reins at Ansham Wolds. Tilliard tapped the pilot on the shoulder.

"Steer oh-nine-oh magnetic please, Bob."

The Lancaster swung into the east, levelled out on the new heading. In the distance the North Sea filled the horizon, and low clouds scudded. The sun was low in the south west, throwing the inside of the cockpit into shadow.

Now for the acid test, a risky variation of the examination Tilliard set every sprog. If Nicholson and his crew got through the next twenty minutes without his having to intervene, they would be deemed 'converted' to Lancasters.

Tilliard flicked his intercom switch. "Feather the starboard outer, please."

"Pilot to crew," Nicholson called, unhesitatingly. "We're about to feather the starboard outer. Stand by for feathering. Out."

He made a thumbs up signal to his Canadian engineer.

Flight Sergeant Rex Preece caught Tilliard's eye, winked. He knew what was going on but then he had flown with his instructor before, at Lindholme. Three months ago Preece had been hospitalised with a broken ankle playing football two days before his original crew went missing over Hanover, coincidentally that was on the same night Bert Fulshawe had died. Only recently restored to the flight roster, Preece had sought out Tilliard and asked his advice.

'Mr Nicholson's looking for an engineer, sir?' He had begun, half-expecting a curt rebuff. 'Only he's a Stirling man. Before I go volunteering I thought I'd like, er, speak to you, sir.'

Tilliard had scowled. The Wingco had had reservations about Bob Nicholson but personally he had hit it off with the man in recent weeks. He honestly believed that Nicholson was an above average pilot.

'Squadron Leader Nicholson is a very able pilot,' he had replied, before relenting a little and permitting himself a lopsided grin. 'If that's what you wanted to know, Preece.' It was exactly what the other man had wanted to know.

Rex Preece and the other five members of Nicholson's all-sergeant crew were about to find out exactly how 'able' their 'Stirling man' was at the controls of a Lancaster.

"Master fuel cock...OFF! Button in...RELEASE BUTTON! Throttle...CLOSED! Slow-running cut-out switch...SET TO IDLE CUT-OFF POSITION!"

Preece craned his neck, checked the Merlin had stopped, confirmed that the propeller was feathered, spinning in the slipstream.

"Number four FEATHERED!"

Nicholson deftly adjusted the throttles to maintain airspeed and altitude on the three remaining engines, applied full trim to the rudder. The manual said a Lancaster was supposed to fly 'feet off' with full rudder trim even with both engines on one side out of commission. However, Tilliard had never found this to be the case in practice. F-Freddie's pilot was having to stand on the left rudder pedal to hold the bomber straight.

F-Freddie droned on into the darkening eastern sky, Merlins purring.

"Navigator," Tilliard intoned. "Plot a heading to take us out to sea over Mablethorpe, please." He waited, Nicholson altered course a few degrees to the south. Several minutes passed. "Instructor to crew," he drawled. "Showtime, gentlemen."

One...two...three...four...five seconds...

Tilliard braced himself, wedged himself fast in the gap behind the pilot's seat, and took one last deep breath.

"FIGHTER PORT!" He screamed at the top of his voice. "CORKSCREW PORT! GO! GO! GO!"

Nicholson threw the Lancaster into a headlong plunge, banking recklessly into a plunging left hand turn as the aircraft fell into space.

"FIGHTER ATTACKING! FOLLOWING US DOWN! CORKSCREW STARBOARD! GO! GO! GO!"

The pilot shoved the three live throttles through the gate, hauled back on the controls, stood on the rudder, wrenched F-Freddie into a stomach churning, gravity-defying wheel to the right. There were curses over the intercom, the airframe groaned in protest, Merlins screamed in the dusk as first the bomber careered one way and then as violently, the other.

Tilliard clung on for dear life.

With one Merlin feathered Nicholson could easily lose control of the bomber. One moment of indecision, one mistake and they would stall, spin, or dive into the cold grey waters far below. An engine problem, any mechanical failure might be fatal. This was flying not so much by the seat of one's pants, as flying along the ragged, jagged crumbling edge of the precipice of a three mile high cliff. Treating a Lanc with a feathered engine like a big Spitfire was *not* a pastime for the faint-hearted. However, if a crew encountered a night fighter over Germany, either the rule book went out of the window or that crew was doomed.

Fighter combats were a bomber pilot's worst nightmare; short, sharp, deadly events. If the gunners saw the fighter first a crew had a single, fleeting opportunity to turn inside the attacking fighter, force it to overshoot and hopefully, lose contact with its prey in the immensity of the night sky. Once a fighter opened fire it was usually too late. A bomber had to corkscrew before it was in a fighter's sights, escape fast or not at all.

"HE'S STILL ON OUR TAIL! CORKSCREW PORT! NOW! NOW!"

Nicholson arrested the steep, diving turn, and sent the Lancaster reeling across the sky in the opposite direction. A week ago Tilliard had despaired of his pupil. Bob had seemed too wedded to the sedate, stately ways of his beloved clumsy Stirlings, incapable of attuning himself to the vastly greater power and manoeuvrability of a Lancaster. It was only in the last couple of days that Nicholson had finally shrugged off his inhibitions, and begun to throw F-Freddie about. It was typical of the man. Outwardly, he was aloof, uneasy in company, a man of decided and firmly, probably implacably held convictions who was never going to be the life and soul of the party. But inwardly, the man possessed a steely resolution. And today, at long last, he was demonstrating it where it mattered the most. In the air, at the controls of a Lancaster.

"I think we've shaken him off, now, Bob," Tilliard decided shortly afterwards, breathless with the terrible excitement which afflicted him at these times. He paused, collected his wits. Now for the icing on the cake. The altimeter read six thousand feet. "Instructor to pilot. Well played, Bob. Okay, I believe the starboard inner may have been damaged by enemy action. I recommend you feather it."

Nicholson hesitated, but only for a moment. He ran his eye over his dials, satisfied himself that his port Merlins were running true.

"Pilot to crew. We're going to feather the starboard inner. Standby, please."

This time F-Freddie's engineer avoided Tilliard's eye. Every man onboard the bomber realised if they had not done so before, that what they had assumed was a normal, routine training exercise, was in fact, in deadly earnest. Both aircraft and crew were being pushed to their limits.

"Jesus," exclaimed one of the gunners over the

intercom. "This is bloody dangerous!"

Tilliard was about to retort that: "It's supposed to be bloody dangerous!" When Bob Nicholson's voice rang in his ears.

"Pilot to crew," he barked. "Everybody will observe intercom discipline. Over!"

Tilliard smiled to himself as Nicholson got on with feathering the starboard inner Merlin.

"Master fuel cock... OFF! Button in... RELEASE BUTTON! Throttle... CLOSED! Slow-running cut-out switch... SET TO IDLE CUT-OFF POSITION! NUMBER THREE FEATHERED, SKIPPER!"

F-Freddie flew easily enough – her bomb bay empty and with three-quarter empty fuel tanks - on two engines although Nicholson had to strain to hold her straight, left leg jammed down hard on the rudder bar.

"I think we'll be okay at this height, Bob." Tilliard remarked to the pilot. "But we'll give the aerobatics a miss for the rest of the trip. At your discretion you may leave the starboard Merlins feathered and head for Waltham Grange, now please. Waltham Grange has been warned to expect us."

Landing on a strange runway on a strange airfield with two feathered Merlins was no joke. That of course, was the point. The punch line. Nicholson craned around, glanced up at him, did not speak. Tilliard pulled off his face mask, breathed in the thin, cold air. He leaned over the pilot's shoulder. Spoke confidentially, quietly almost into Nicholson's right ear. This was for the pilot's hearing, and his alone.

"You are officially 'converted' to Lancs, Bob. Congratulations." He patted the pilot's shoulder and the two men exchanged a nod of mutual respect.

"Pilot to navigator. Give me a heading for Waltham Grange."

Chapter 22

Wednesday 22nd December, 1943
RAF Waltham Grange, Lincolnshire

Squadron Leader Clive Irving winced as the Lancaster bounced drunkenly down his runway. Notwithstanding a gusting northerly cross wind, Peter Tilliard's pupil had elected to land on two engines.

Clot!

Peter must think the fellow driving that Lanc must be pretty damned top-notch letting him try a stunt like that. But Peter was a good judge of these things; in fact, he was probably the best he had ever come across.

'No problem, Peter,' Irving had replied when his old friend from Lindholme had telephoned him that morning with his odd request. 'Just make sure the bugger doesn't block my runway!'

'If we have a crash it won't be anywhere near your precious runway!' Tilliard had retorted, laughing.

'That's okay then!'

Irving watched the Lancaster roll onto the perimeter road, stepped up into the cab of the Bedford and waved the WAAF driver to carry on. The truck jolted across the field to meet the taxiing bomber. He had heard via the grapevine that Peter had had a bad re-introduction to ops at Ansham Wolds but that things had looked up after Bert Fulshawe's 'accident'. He saw Adam Chantrey's hand in that, as he saw his hand in so much that still went on at Waltham Grange, three months after his departure. When the Wingco discovered he had a Lindholme instructor on his Squadron he would have treated Peter like gold dust, taken him under his wing.

Erks were wedging chocks under F-Freddie's big, fat wheels when the WAAF parked the Bedford under the starboard wing tip of the bomber. Irving walked to the rear of the aircraft. It was freezing in the wintery twilight and his breath frosted in his face. The forecast for tomorrow was for clear weather. Tomorrow they would go back to war. Today he would renew acquaintance with an old friend.

Tilliard was the first man through the fuselage door, tossing out a bag and jumping down after it. He beamed broadly, strode over and clasped Irving's outstretched hand.

"Clive! Goodness, it's marvellous to see you again!"

"You too, old man! A Flight Commander, then?"

"And you've got your own squadron!"

Irving chuckled. "Fortunes of war, and so forth."

"Nevertheless," Tilliard insisted. "I think congratulations are in order." Their gaze met, briefly. Only briefly, it was all they dared. Any longer and there might have been tears in their eyes for the all the fine fellows they had known at Lindholme, and since. They were superbly well-practised in veiling their emotions. Tilliard was glad when he sensed a presence at his shoulder.

"Clive, let me introduce you to Bob Nicholson."

F-Freddie's pilot nodded wordlessly, unsmilingly

to Irving.

"Bob has just qualified on Lancs," Tilliard went on. "Although, the next time you bounce a kite up and down like that, I think I'll watch from a safe distance, old man!"

This prompted a thin smile on Nicholson's lips.

"I'm a Stirling man at heart," he explained, relaxing. "Peter's had his work cut out teaching this particular old dog how to shake a new bone, I'm afraid."

"Well, judging by that landing you seem to have got the hang of it!" Irving assured him, eying the sky. The late afternoon mists were gathering over the low, flat fields of the flood plains of the River Trent. "You're very welcome to be my guest in the Mess tonight, Bob."

"Thank you. I plan to return to Ansham Wolds, directly."

"As you wish."

"Bit of a cold fish?" Irving remarked to Tilliard as they drove back to the Mess, leaving Nicholson and his crew running up F-Freddie's Merlins in the gathering darkness.

"Bob's a decent enough fellow," his friend said. "He'll be okay once he's got a few ops under his belt. Been away a tad too long, that's all."

"Oh, right. Stirling man, he said?"

"Afraid so."

"Poor sod. Still, there are worse things."

Tilliard grunted. "Like flying Halifaxes these days," he observed.

"Wouldn't fancy it, myself," Irving agreed.

Last night the Halifax Force had taken another beating on the way to Frankfurt. One in ten of the

Halifaxes despatched had failed to return, 27 aircraft. In comparison, the much larger Lancaster Force had lost only 14 of its number, a chop rate of a mere three-and-a-half percent.

"Still, nobody lives forever, what!"

Tilliard started laughing.

"Now what have I said?" Irving demanded.

"Nothing. It's just the way you said it. You sounded just like the Wingco."

The WAAF driver stared ahead into the dusk, the Bedford roared and creaked over the ground and night was falling fast over Lincolnshire.

A mile away F-Freddie thundered down the runway; hauled into the air and set a course for home.

Chapter 23

Wednesday 22nd December, 1943
The Gatekeeper's Lodge, Ansham Wolds, Lincolnshire

Candles flickered, the light played on their faces and glinted in their eyes. The warmth of the range filled the kitchen. The bewitching company of the woman he loved, and her cooking washed down with several glasses of the Rector's cloudy blackberry wine had put Adam almost completely at his ease. He viewed Eleanor sleepily across the table and she smiled back at him. Upstairs her father slept, peacefully, drugged now with laudanum. The children were long in their beds, but not before they had come and said their goodnights to the man in their mother's life. The small family was drawing in upon itself and Adam increasingly felt himself to be a part of it, content within its circle.

The Prof was fading fast. The doctor had called that evening, taken Adam aside and explained that there was nothing to be done. Nature would now take its course, it was only a matter of days. Possibly hours.

Eleanor's strength humbled Adam. She remained cheerful, brave always, as if she was determined that come Hell or high water she would not mourn her father while he still lived. While he lived she clung to the joy in her life, and refused to yield to her inner grief. Even though the end was near, she was calm. Almost serene.

Adam recounted Bob Nicholson's tumble in the Mess, the chaos of the racing cycles. She laughed, made no comment although she raised an eyebrow when he let slip that Peter Tilliard had taken the squadron's second-in-command on a 'rather fierce corkscrew run' that afternoon.

"It is how we find out if a chap's converted to type. In Bob's case, converted from Stirlings to Lancs. If a chap comes through it then he's passed fit for ops. It's sort of kill or cure."

"Oh," she murmured, intrigued.

"Mac says Peter takes a malicious pleasure in thinking up new surprises for each crew." He leaned forward, rested his elbows on the table and his chin on his clasped hands. "Would you like me to stay tonight? The Prof being the way he is."

Eleanor shook her head.

"No. I shall be all right. Honestly." She reached out, took his hand. "I shall be all right. There's nothing either of us can do. You must get your sleep. We must both be practical about things, darling."

Adam nodded.

"Why haven't you asked Eleanor to marry you?" The old man had asked him. That was the last time he had spoken to the Prof, the last time the old man was coherent, the last time he was truly in the land of the living. The question never really went away but in honour he could do no more than hold it in abeyance.

It was the war.

It was just the bloody war.

"I think you're very brave," he said, fondly.

Eleanor lowered her eyes for a moment.

"No, I'm not. Not at all, really," she replied, squeezing his hand and making to rise. "I must clear the plates away."

Adam rose, stepped around the table and wrapped her in his arms. The gloom enveloped them as he rocked her slowly, while softly she wept on his shoulder.

That morning, burying the seven sprogs killed on Black Thursday in the shadow of St Paul's ancient church tower, he had felt nothing other than an impatience to have the rites properly, decently observed. The dead were dead, gone. Black Thursday was history, swiftly, pragmatically relegated to Bomber Command folklore. His crews had returned safely from Frankfurt; that was what was important. Burying sprogs was something a Squadron Commander got used to early on. It happened a lot, it was the way of the world. There was no point getting broody over sprogs. Sprogs came and went, sprogs were nobody's friends. The main thing was that the crews had bounced back from last week's nightmare in the fog and pressed on to Frankfurt. Pressing on, that was the ticket. Never mind the fact the Pathfinders had put down their markers in open country several miles southeast of the target. Never mind that the Main Force had dropped two thousand tons of ordnance on nothing in particular. Dead sprogs and cock ups were occupational hazards. All that was left was to carry on, to get on with the job.

Eleanor was quiescent in his arms, sobbing quietly.

"Do you know what the oddest thing is?" She said, sniffing.

"No?"

"Despite everything, these last few days I've been so happy." He planted a kiss in her hair. "And I feel so guilty. I ought to be with father." They stepped apart. The woman smoothed down her dress, the man straightened his battledress.

"I'll sit with you awhile, if I may."

Chapter 24

Wednesday 22nd December, 1943
RAF Waltham Grange, Lincolnshire

Suzy was thinking of Peter Tilliard. She had not written him a proper letter since her arrival at Waltham Grange. There was so much going on, too much to do, and so much to learn. She was weary, longed to lie down on her cot and sleep even though it was still early and later there was a dance in the Mess which she felt duty bound to go to that night. She desperately wanted to avoid giving the impression she was being offish; wanted to fit in, to be 'one of the girls' in a way that she had never been at Ansham Wolds. Peter had saved her from herself at Ansham Wolds. He had helped her grow up in a rush. Helped her to put behind her the girlish things of childhood.

The knock at the door made her start.
"There's somebody asking for you downstairs."
"Who?"
"They didn't say."

With a sigh Suzy put down her pen, buttoned her tunic. On her way out she paused at the mirror, checked her hair was turned up, bobbed off her shoulders as per regulations, and that her sparsely applied makeup was not smudged. The Waafery was quiet and her steps rang out on the wooden floor. There was nobody in the lobby at the end of the corridor.

"I was told there was somebody to see me?" She asked, irritably.

"There is, ma'am," returned the WAAF at the desk. "*He's* waiting outside, ma'am."

"Oh."

Suzy went outside, into the darkness and the cold. It was a moment before her eyes adjusted to the night.

"Suzy!"

At the sound of the man's voice she spun around. And there he was, his cap tilted at a rakish angle, sheepskin flying jacket slung casually over his shoulder, tall, handsome and smiling, and walking towards her.

"Peter!" Suzy ran to him and threw her arms around his neck. He hugged her, lifted her off her feet. "Peter! Peter!"

He laughed, put her down.

"I've missed you terribly," the man exclaimed.

"Oh, and I've missed you so!" It was over seven weeks since they had set eyes on each other. They had grown up as many years in those weeks. Become different people, no longer the fumbling, uncertain innocents of the autumn.

"It's a tad public, here," Tilliard murmured as a pair of WAAFs tripped up the steps and into the Waafery. "Perhaps, we could go for a walk?"

Suzy nodded. The man draped his big, heavy, warm sheepskin jacket about her slender shoulders, took her hand in his, guided her into the gloom between the huts.

"Whatever are you doing here, darling?"

"Clive Irving and I were together at Lindholme," he told her. "So I thought I'd look him up and congratulate him on getting his own squadron."

Suzy stopped dead in her tracks.

"Was that your kite that made that awful landing this afternoon?"

"In a manner of speaking," he explained, tongue in cheek. "Actually, Bob Nicholson, 647's new second-in-command was flying. A little training jaunt. The grand finale was putting down on two engines. Nobody got killed," he chuckled, "so he passed muster."

"You shouldn't take so many risks!"

Tilliard drew her into the shadows.

"Sorry, no can do."

"Not even for me?"

"That's not fair."

"Isn't it?"

"You know it isn't. Because I love you, Suzy Mills," he declared, gently, vehemently. They kissed in the gloom. Kiss followed kiss, then breathlessly they clung together, shocked by themselves.

"Oh, dear," Suzy muttered. "What would people think if they saw us now?"

"They'd probably think we were lovers."

"And they'd be right."

"Clive tells me there's a do in the Mess tonight?"

"A dance," she said, eyes shining brightly.

"Or we could go up to Lincoln?"

"No," Suzy decided with a sudden certainty. "We don't have to hide anything. Not anymore. Not here."

"It's the dance, then. But I warn you I'm a bit of a dunce on the dance floor." They walked in a wide circle around the Waafery. "Jack Gordon's engaged to Nancy Bowman, by the way," the man announced.

"Never!"

Tilliard filled her in on the whole story.

"Oh," Suzy laughed, nervily. "There but for the grace of god, and all that, darling," she reminded him. "No," she hurried on before he asked. "I don't think we've got anything to worry about. Although we were awfully, well, reckless."

He did not know what to say.

"But it was lovely, wasn't it?" Suzy whispered, happily.

This deepened his embarrassment further and reduced him to shambling incoherence.

"Absolutely..."

"So how did Jack get hurt?"

"Jack was in the astrodome," he stuttered, lamely. "Nothing to hold onto when we corkscrewed. When you corkscrew everything that's not tied down gets chucked around the kite. Jack got bounced around a bit."

Suzy did not pursue the subject. The man she loved had spent Thursday night dicing with a fighter over Germany. It was no good thinking about these things, it was the stuff of nightmares. She was surprised when he blurted out more.

"Tom Dennison bought it! Cannon shell. Damn nearly cut him in half. Jack kept him alive until we got back but they couldn't do anything for him at the base hospital. We tried to get him up to Hull yesterday. He died on the way. I haven't had the heart to tell Jack yet. He'll take it badly."

Suzy remembered Tom Dennison.

A laughing boy with a mop of red hair, usually with a cigarette drooping from his lips. He could not have been more than twenty or twenty-one. He had courted a plain girl from Huddersfield in the typing pool, who had steadfastly, coldly repulsed his every advance. She recalled that nothing seemed to stop the wireless operator from smiling, not even the frigid cold shoulder of the comely WAAF who preferred the attentions of Canadian aircrew, whose pay was twice that of their RAF comrades.

In normal times she might have despised the girl in the typing pool, no matter that to do so would have been pure hypocrisy. Times were anything but normal. For all she knew they were living in the last days of the world. Or at any rate, the last days of the world her parents had known, of the world into which she had been born, certainly the last days of the world in which she had grown up. Suzy had made her own choices: fallen in love with a Lancaster pilot, given herself to him body and soul regardless of the costs. That was her choice; if another woman made another choice, then that was her business.

"You must tell Jack before he hears it from somebody else, darling."

The man nodded.

"I'll go down to the *Hare and Hounds* tomorrow, as soon as I get back."

"How will you get back?"

"As long as we're not on for tomorrow, Clive's offered to ferry me up to Ansham Wolds. Sort of a reciprocal visit, a social call on Wing-Commander Chantrey."

Suzy noted the resilience in him, how quickly he had shrugged off his melancholy, put it to one side. That was an aircrew trait, something the old lags cultivated, developed to a fine art. She was relieved, Peter was still Peter. *Her* Peter.

"They still think very highly of Wing-Commander Chantrey here."

Tilliard put his arm about her.

"Clive was saying you've had a bit of a bad run, lately."

"A bit. What's it been like back at Ansham Wolds."

"Dicey. I think it's the same everywhere. Of course, it's worse for the Halifaxes." The increasingly desperate plight of the Halifax squadrons since the withdrawal of the last Stirlings was the worst kept secret in Bomber Command. "Still, that's the way it goes, I suppose. Anyway, that's enough talking shop. When are they going to let you have some leave?"

"I've only just got here!"

"Detail. I want you to myself. That's not too much to ask, is it?"

"No," she giggled, laying her head against his shoulder, shrugging the sheepskins close about herself. "I might be able to wangle a day or two off the station sometime next month. I don't know. Things are, well, hectic. You know."

"Yes, I know. Well, at least now that you're back in One Group country we can actually get to see each other once in a while without breaking King's regs. The last few weeks it has been as if we were at the opposite ends of the earth."

"We're together now."

"Yes, that's the main thing."

Chapter 25

Thursday 23rd December, 1943
RAF Waltham Grange, Lincolnshire

"Two engines in a cross wind?" The Wingco queried cheerfully when Peter Tilliard had spoken to him that morning on the scrambler line from Waltham Grange. "Yes, I should imagine it was a bit bouncy. But so far as you're concerned Bob's qualified on Lancs? With flying colours? That's excellent news. No, I haven't seen him yet today. I should think he's pretty chuffed, though. Yes, it looks as if we're on for tonight. Right, Bob can lead us off then. Good work, Peter."

Tilliard explained he was going to hitch a lift back to Ansham Wolds but the Wingco put his foot down.

"Oh, no you don't, old man! You're long overdue a spot of leave. Take seventy-two hours. You're not indispensable, you know!"

"I've a hundred things to do, sir!" Tilliard protested. "Probably more!"

The Wingco's mind was already made up.

"Nonsense! I've just had the forecast for the next few days. Storms, rain, wind, perhaps a bit of snow. After tonight's show the Chief's not going to be looking for another fight for at least two or three days!"

"Yes, sir," he had conceded. "But..."

"No buts, Peter. I don't want to see your face for three days. Spend some time with that lovely WAAF of yours!"

This had brought Tilliard up short. The heat rose in his cheeks. The Wingco knew about Suzy! There was an awkward silence at the Waltham Grange end of the line, then: "Oh, you know about Suzy, sir?"

"I had a little chinwag with Clive Irving last night and he happened to remark that you seemed to be spending an inordinate amount of time on the dance floor with a 'damned pretty little thing' who had come from my 'part of the world'. The Adjutant and I put one and one together and came up with the name of a certain newly commissioned assistant section officer. Am I on the right track?"

"Yes, sir."

"Good for you!" The Wingco clearly thought it was all very amusing. "Spend some time with her, Peter," he laughed. "And that's an order!" With which he hung up.

"Three days?" Clive Irving had winked, knowingly.

"Three days," Tilliard confirmed, realising that the Wingco and his host at Waltham Grange were in league against him. Ranged against such formidable foes he gave in, accepted the situation gracefully. "No chance of hitching a lift tonight, I suppose?"

His optimistic inquiry was greeted with a blanket refusal.

"Not a chance, old man!"

"Fair enough. I'm on leave then."

"Got it in one," Irving beamed, broadly. "Any ideas what you'll do?"

"I'll hang around here, if that's okay?"

"Capital!"

Tilliard had said his farewells to Suzy in the dark behind the Waafery around midnight, not expecting to see her again for some weeks. The Operations Room teleprinter was clattering up the preliminary battle order for the coming evening's entertainment as Tilliard sauntered into the bunker.

Suzy blinked up from her work, surprised, pleased.

"Peter," she whispered, looking about herself, anxiously.

"I had a word with the Ops Officer, he said it would be alright for me to interrupt you. For a minute or so," he explained lowly. He led her away to the doorway, where, a little removed from the hustle and bustle, they looked one to the other, uncomfortably. In the background the teleprinter rattled loudly, unceasingly.

"What are you doing here?" She asked.

"The Wingco's told me to take seventy-two hours leave. No ifs, no buts. I shall be a guest of the Mess over Christmas, it would seem."

"That's marvellous news."

"Yes."

Neither of them knew what to say next.

Tilliard coughed, cleared his throat.

"I'd better let you get back. Ramsey seems a decent sort, but I won't overstay my welcome. I don't want to get you into trouble..."

"No, of course not."

"I'll see you later, perhaps?"

"Yes."

Tilliard had gone back to the Mess, read a paper from cover to cover for the first time in months, eaten lunch alone, gone for a walk, then returned again to the Mess. He felt at a loose end, useless. A spare part. Separate from things, fretting about his crews back at Ansham Wolds, about a dozen other things over which he had no control while all around him Waltham Grange gathered itself to launch its heavies against the Big City.

"Stop looking so bloody sorry for yourself!" Clive Irving declared, finding his friend brooding in a corner of the Mess. "You'll be late for the main crew briefing if you don't get weaving."

It was the first time Tilliard had ever attended a briefing as an observer, albeit a far from disinterested observer. He sat at the back of the hall, shrank into the shadows, wishing he was going with the crews to Berlin.

Tonight's operation was an all-Lancaster affair. Maximum effort, all squadrons. Nearly 500 Lancs had been available for the last Berlin raid, but tonight a week after Black Thursday, less than 400 hundred aircraft would be in the air. Nevertheless, Bomber Command was carting another 1,500 tons of high explosives and incendiaries to the German capital. This, despite the fact that the long, southerly approach to Berlin threatening both Frankfurt and Leipzig required maximum fuel loads.

Tilliard lapsed into his thoughts as the briefing progressed. 8 Group Mosquitoes were mounting small diversionary attacks on Aachen, Duisburg and Leipzig. The normal drill. Over the target the Pathfinders would employ the latest refinement of the now standard 'Berlin Method'. He picked up his ears when a new innovation was promulgated.

Each Squadron had been asked to nominate two experienced navigators to act as 'wind finders'. These navigators would calculate the actual winds they encountered on the route out and broadcast their 'found winds' back to Command at regular intervals. These 'found winds' would then be averaged, and re-broadcast to the Main Force over Germany.

"This is a bloody good idea!" Clive Irving declared. "If everybody uses the 'found winds' over Germany the bomber stream ought to be a bloody site tighter tonight than it has been on the last few shows. It should also mean that you sprogs have got much less excuse for getting lost!"

Waltham Grange was despatching 14 aircraft, including three in the hands of sprog crews making their operational debuts. Light winds and scattered cloud was forecast over the target. Take off was scheduled for the early evening.

However, all afternoon the clouds built up over Lincolnshire. Rain fell, the wind began to gust, fitfully at first, and then beneath a lowering overcast, hard out of the west as cookies and canisters of incendiaries were winched into the gaping bellies of the Squadron's heavies. With less than an hour to go, takeoff was postponed and as the light failed across the stormy airfield, most assumed that it was only a matter of time before the operation was scrubbed.

"We should just bloody well go!" Clive Irving fumed.

Having donned full cold-weather flying kit he stomped about the flight room like an enraged grizzly bear for some minutes, then accepted the inevitable. He changed back into battledress, and set about "geeing up the chaps". From long and bitter experience of such situations, he was taking nothing for granted. The order to reschedule the off could come at any time.

"This weather might blow over in an hour or two," Tilliard offered, cautiously.

"Better to go now than have to come back in daylight!"

Delays were evil things.

Tilliard said nothing.

Chapter 26

Thursday 23rd December, 1943
RAF Ansham Wolds, Lincolnshire

The flight sergeant fitter handed the pilot of Lancaster M-Mother Form 700 on a grubby clipboard at twenty-five minutes to midnight.

"Thank you, Riggs," Adam grunted, scrawling his signature.

Ben ducked his bear-like frame under the open bomb bay doors, solemnly patted the cold rounded flank of the cookie, and emerged again into the open air. Taffy Davies stood by the tail plane, concentrated hard and urinated on the tail wheel. Ted Hallowes walked under the wing, reached up and touched the tip of one of the three great flukes of the bomber's starboard inner Merlin. Bob Marshall and Bert Pound looked at each other, took one last drag on their cigarettes, dropped them on the damp tarmac and as one man, ground them out underfoot. Angus Robertson watched the performance of each ritual in silence.

"Permission to mount up, sir?"

Adam smiled in the night.

"Lead the way, Round Again." The preparatory rites had to be observed. Every little bit helped, especially when the Lancaster Force was operating alone against the Big City. In a few minutes it would be Christmas Eve. Hostilities did not stop for Christmas. Nobody was playing football in no man's land in this war. In four hours the first of hundreds of cookies would be falling on Berlin.

There was deep snow on the ground in Germany. In Russia the flames of burning Tigers signposted the road to Berlin. In Italy the British Eighth Army, and the American Fifth were fighting their way towards Rome. Hitler's Reich was shrinking; everywhere the Wehrmacht was digging in, fighting savagely to hold the line. In Germany, the great cities of the Fatherland lay in ruins, burned out shells, their citizens living like so many sewer rats in the rubble. It was the fifth Christmas of the war and between winter storms the Main Force was hammering at the gates of *Grosse Deutschland.*

Settling at the controls of M-Mother, Adam took a deep breath. He had almost survived another year. Be satisfied with that, he told himself. This was not the time to ask how or why he had survived. When in moments of weakness he was tempted to believe that fate was anything but blind, he remembered the regiment of the dead and the maimed, the captive and the unhinged, the friends gone forever and the countless sprogs that *he* personally had sacrificed to the mill of ops. There was no guiding hand watching over him. There was no God. No such thing as manifest destiny. There was only the next op.

Ted Hallowes started calling down the engine checklist. It focussed Adam's mind on the task in hand. The drill gripped him, shut out distractions. The cause was just, Adam repeated privately. Over and over again. *The cause is just. The cause is just. The cause is just...*

Yes, the cause was just and that was enough.
More than enough.

At the appointed hour the green flare climbed high above the airfield, Lancasters jolted out onto the perimeter road, and filed clumsily around to the threshold of the main runway.

Adam advanced the throttles to zero boost against the brakes. In the distance he saw the first Lancaster's navigation lights winking as it climbed. Bob Nicholson, having passed Peter Tilliard's 'corkscrew run' with flying colours the previous day had been given the honour of leading off the Squadron in F-Freddie. Adam throttled back. M-Mother's Merlins purred in the night, the aircraft hummed and shook, straining in the slips, eager for the battle.

"Green light, Skipper!" Ted Hallowes called.

"Pilot to rear gunner. All clear behind?"

"Rear gunner to pilot. All clear behind, Skipper!" Taffy Davies barked.

Adam advanced the throttles, holding the bomber on the brakes. At zero boost he released the brakes and with a hiss, the Lancaster rolled forward. Ahead the flare path stretched into the darkness, a mile long corridor of light across the top of the high wold. A touch of the brakes and the tail came up.

Hallowes was shouting speeds. "Eighty... Eighty-five... Ninety... Ninety-five..." M-Mother thundered down the flare path, roaring, shaking, rocking under his hands. "One hundred... And Five... One-one-oh... One-one-five..." The aircraft wanted to fly, unstick, soar free of the ground. "One-twenty..." Adam eased the controls towards his midriff. M-Mother flew.

Chapter 27

Thursday 23rd December, 1943
RAF Waltham Grange, Lincolnshire

The Lancaster Force had eventually set off for Berlin seven hours late. By then the wind and rain had relented and the night was clear. Far out in the Atlantic the next storm system was approaching out of the west. This time tomorrow the weather would have closed in completely, possibly for several days. Gales, even snow was forecast. Tonight's attack might be the last of the year and come Hell or high water, it had been decreed that it would go ahead.

The first wave was scheduled to bomb at 03:58.

Tilliard stood in the crowd beside the main runway. He huddled in his sheepskins, yearned to be riding with the Main Force. Ached for anything but this feeling of helplessness. He did not belong at Waltham Grange; his place was at Ansham Wolds. Loneliness settled about him and like the cold it ate into him, slowly eroding his belief in the rightness of things, sapping his strength and his will.

"Hello, stranger."

The man turned, Suzy smiled.

The harsh glare of the flare path lights glistened in her eyes.

"Hello, there," he muttered, caught unawares in his thoughts.

"I thought I'd find you here." She threaded her arm through his.

"Force of habit," he grimaced. "I don't like to miss an off."

"No. Neither do I."

C-Charlie lurched up to the threshold. Her pilot advanced the throttles against the brakes, throttled back, waited for the signal to roll. In the distance R-Robert unstuck, hauled into the night, navigation lights winking through the spray. A cheer erupted, C-Charlie was rolling, Merlins picking up.

"Isn't it just our luck," Suzy said. "The first time we're together and Command decides to despatch the Lancaster Force to the Big City!"

"Isn't it just."

"Cheer up," she chided him, gently, wearily. "After tonight, it looks like we'll be stood down for ages."

C-Charlie swept past them. More bombers were lumbering into position, queueing along the perimeter road, Merlins idling in the stillness of the night. The air trembled with the rumbling heartbeat of the Main Force. High overhead, countless aircraft were climbing over Lincolnshire, setting course into the south-east and the faraway convergence point over the North Sea.

Tilliard glanced at Suzy.

For a moment he was torn: a part of him was flying with 647 Squadron's Lancasters; a part of him utterly lost in her. Nothing made much sense any more, confusion ruled. It was as if he was two men, one in conflict with the other. It was Christmas and the Main Force was off to Germany to wreak dreadful havoc in the streets of Berlin. It was Christmas and beyond all expectations he was reunited with the woman he loved. The contradictions of his life haunted him, haunted him as they had never done before, haunted him as he had never imaged they could or ever would. He looked into Suzy's shining eyes and he felt guilty. Guilty to be alive while so many others were dead, guilty for what he had and so many other men would never have. Guilty for having so much joy in his life when all around him was the wreckage of the world.

"What is it, darling?" Suzy asked, leaning against him.

He swallowed, hard.

"Too much time to think," he murmured, shrugging.

The next Lancaster, L-London, was rolling.

"Never mind," she soothed. "At least we're together for Christmas, darling."

Chapter 28

Tuesday 28th December, 1943
St. Pauls Church, Ansham Wolds, Lincolnshire

Eleanor's father was buried on a cold, bleak winter day beneath a leaden sky. The old man had died as the Lancaster Force had flown away from Berlin in the small hours of Friday morning, Christmas Eve. Adam stood with Eleanor and the children. Across the open grave Air Commodore Crowe-Martin was flanked by Group Captain Alexander, 647 Squadron's Flight Commanders and most of the station's senior officers. A large contingent from the village had filed up the hill, and packed the narrow oaken pews of the ancient Norman church. The Deputy Group Commander had paid the Prof a brief, heartfelt tribute during the service.

'I first met Charles Merry many years ago. Present circumstances do not permit me to do full justice to the great contribution that Professor Merry's tireless work has made to the winning of this war. Suffice it to say his work has saved countless of our young men's lives, and will continue to do so in future. 'The Prof', as we all knew him, had a brilliant and inventive mind and the courage to fight to ensure that his ideas were not only heard, but acted upon both in the Air Ministry, and within the higher echelons of Bomber Command. It is my heartfelt hope that, when the war is over, historians will ensure he is accorded the credit and the honour he never sought for himself in life but he so justly deserves...'

Adam pressed Eleanor's hand.

M-Mother had lost a Merlin on the bomb run over Berlin, limped back at low level, and put down at Wyton, an 8 Group station. It had taken all day to patch up the aircraft, delaying his return to Ansham Wolds until evening. Eleanor had been left to cope on her own. Everybody had rallied around, not least the Rector, his wife and the Station Master. Johnny and Emmy had been taken in by the Bowmans at the *Sherwood Arms*; and Adelaide Naismith-Parry had stayed the night with Eleanor.

Group Captain Alexander had taken Adam aside on his return, breaking the news of the Prof's death and assuring him that Eleanor was not alone.

'Eleanor is bearing up and she understands that you have your duties here. So, let's not have you blaming yourself for not being on the spot, and all that nonsense.'

On Christmas Day the officers went to the other ranks' messes, acted as canteen orderlies, serving the non-commissioned personnel their Christmas Dinner. Adam led his officers, took the cheers and the banter of the occasion with a large pinch of salt, laughed and smiled, played the role he knew he had to play. It was night before he eventually got away from the station, drove down to the village and knocked on the door of the Gatekeeper's Lodge. The wind had rustled through the gaunt branches of the trees, a chill rain was falling.

'I was with him when he went,' Eleanor told him, quietly. She had stopped crying, for the while. She was pale, drained, and her hands shook gently. 'It was very peaceful. He sort of sighed, and was gone. I don't think he was in any pain. I looked at him for a long time. I checked to see if he had a pulse. There wasn't. So I sat with him until it was light. I covered him up. Then I took the children around to the Bowmans and went to see Simon at the Rectory. Everybody's been marvellous. But I wish they'd leave me alone. I shall be fine, but I need a little time alone and it's so hard getting people to understand that. One doesn't want to seem ungrateful, everybody's been so kind. So very, very kind.'

He had sat her on his lap, cradled her in his arms until she slept. The Rector and his wife had found them this way in the parlour later that evening, smiled and tiptoed through to the kitchen. Adam listened to the Naismith-Parry's moving around, Adelaide filling the kettle, stoking the range.

'Eleanor must have something to eat,' the old lady whispered, creeping back into the parlour. 'I shall make a pot of tea.'

Adam nodded, Eleanor stirred but did not wake.

'How are Johnny and Emmy?'

'I don't think they know what's happening. Not yet,' replied the Reverend Naismith-Parry. 'We thought we'd let them have Christmas Day. Before we tried to explain.'

Now as Adam held Eleanor's hand at the grave side, Christmas Day seemed an age ago. The children had cried when Eleanor told them their grandfather was dead, gone forever. Perhaps, they wept their tears because they saw their mother crying? Perhaps, they cried because they understood enough about death to grieve? Adam had tried to explain to Johnny that when somebody died, the main thing was for the living to carry on. That it was good to mourn, to miss the dead but that life had to go on even though memories could be very painful. He had assumed the role of the boy's dead father and it was a little frightening, daunting.

"*Man that is born of woman hath but a short time to live,*" intoned the Rector, his voice strained, "*and is full of misery. He cometh up, and is cut down, like a flower; he fleeth as it were a shadow, and never continueth in one stay.*"

They were burying the Prof in a grave immediately adjacent to the Grafton family plot, next to the fresh, clean stone crosses which marked the last resting places of the sprogs killed on Black Thursday. One way and another, the old man was in good company.

"*In the midst of life we are in death: of whom may we seek for succour, but of thee, O Lord, who for our sins art justly displeased. Yet, O Lord God most holy, O Lord most mighty, O holy and most merciful Saviour, deliver us not into the bitter pains of eternal death.*"

The Group Commander had sent Eleanor a personal, hand-written note apologising for not being able to attend her father's funeral. The AOC had said that her father would be greatly missed and had made 'an immeasurable contribution to the cause of victory.'

"*Thou knowest, Lord, the secrets of our hearts; shut not thy merciful ears to our prayer; but spare us, Lord most holy, O God most mighty, O holy and merciful Saviour, thou most worthy judge eternal, suffer us not, at our last hour, for any pains of death, to fall from thee."*

As the coffin was lowered into the ground the Reverend Naismith-Parry wearily stooped to pick up a handful of earth.

"Forasmuch as it hath pleased Almighty God of his great mercy to take unto himself the soul of our dear brother here departed, we therefore commit his body to the ground; earth to earth, ashes to ashes, dust to dust; in sure and certain hope of the Resurrection to eternal life, through our Lord Jesus Christ; who shall change our vile body, that it may be like unto his glorious body, according to the mighty working, whereby he is able to subdue all things to himself."

Adam raised his head.

"Our Father, which art in Heaven, Hallowed be thy name. Thy kingdom come. Thy will be done, in earth as it is in Heaven. Give us this day our daily bread. And forgive us our trespasses. As we forgive them that trespass against us. And lead us not into temptation; but deliver us from evil."

"Amen," he thought.

Tea, scones and biscuits awaited the mourners in the Church Hall. The rain rattled on the corrugated iron roof as Eleanor circulated, making certain she spoke to as many people as possible. She held back her tears, put on her bravest face.

"The AOC had planned to come down this morning," Air Commodore Crowe-Martin confided to Adam. "But it was not possible. Something came up. He always regarded the Prof with the utmost respect, you know."

"So I gather, sir."

"I hear Bob Nicholson broke his duck last week?"

"Yes, sir."

"Capital fellow. He's been pining to get back on ops for months, you know."

"I can imagine."

The Deputy Group Commander had fixed the younger man in his steely stare, taken him by the arm. He lowered his voice. "Charles will have taken great comfort from knowing that Eleanor has a chap like you to look after her. Great comfort."

Adam felt the heat rise in his cheeks.

"Er, thank you, sir."

"Air Commodore," Eleanor said, materialising by Adam's shoulder. "I haven't had an opportunity to thank you for what you said earlier in the church. It was very moving. Thank you."

"Stephen," smiled the dapper, fox-like Deputy AOC. "You must call me Stephen. I can't have the Prof's daughter standing on ceremony. I won't have it, my dear."

"Stephen, then," Eleanor conceded, smiling briefly. "I hope Adam hasn't got you talking shop."

"If we are, it's my fault. I apologise, but the thing is I know I can always rely on your young man here to give me an honest answer to an honest question. And believe me, that's quite rare these days!"

"And no doubt rather disconcerting?" Eleanor observed, wryly.

"Somewhat," agreed the Deputy AOC. "I thought it all went very well today. I know this isn't perhaps the right time to say it. But I'm sure you two young people will be very happy together. It's not often one sees a couple who are so well matched."

Adam coughed, uneasily. Eleanor meanwhile, smiled sweetly, demurely.

"Er, thank you, sir," muttered the man.

Shortly afterwards, the Deputy AOC made his excuses and departed with Group Captain Alexander.

In the middle of the afternoon Adam walked Eleanor and the children back to the Gatekeeper's Lodge. Eleanor had wanted to stay to help clear up at the Church Hall, Adelaide Naismith-Parry and Betty Bowman would hear none of it.

"You let the Wing-Commander take you home, dear. You leave this to us. You're tired out."

They took the path through the wintery woods, with Johnny and Emmy kicking up the leaves. The children were subdued from the events of the day, otherwise they were their normal selves.

"Why did father want you court-martialled?" Eleanor asked as they walked. "It bothered him," she prompted. "I know how important it was to him that he was able to make his peace with you."

Adam composed himself.

"Last year about a month before I took over at Waltham Grange 388 Squadron was equipped with an experimental electronic 'fighter warning' device. Almost as soon as the devices were fitted the Squadron's chop rate doubled. The sets were acting like homing beacons. I tried to get the trial halted. Through channels, at first. When that didn't work, I ordered the kit stripped out of my kites. The Squadron's chop rate fell immediately. The Prof's *people* weren't terribly happy. I'd wrecked their trial, you see. The Prof probably felt he had to back up *his* people, so he demanded somebody's head. I just happened to be the man on the spot. It wasn't personal. These things go on all the time. It's how we learn, trial and error. Because some of my chaps bought it, a lot of other chaps are probably still alive today. Technical innovation is like that. Two steps forward, one back. One day you get a bit of an advantage over the other fellow, the next day he catches up, or maybe he overtakes you. Then you catch up again, and hope against hope he won't see through your latest wheeze. So it goes on. Like a circle. Round and round again."

"But you almost got court-martialled?"

"There are worse things."

They walked on, very slowly, now. The woman leaned on him.

Eleanor blinked at him, moist eyed.

"Did you blame father for the death of your crews?"

Adam stopped, pressed her hand.

"No. I blamed myself. I was in command. They were *my* crews flying under *my* orders. So," he shrugged, spoke quietly. "I blamed myself. I always blame myself. I couldn't look myself in the eye in the mirror otherwise. No, I didn't blame the Prof then, and I don't blame him now. And that's an end of it, my love."

Chapter 29

Wednesday 29th December, 1943
RAF Waltham Grange, Lincolnshire

Suzy shivered. There was frost in the night air, and the scent of snow. Around the airfield the thunder of Merlins reverberated as the Squadron's Lancasters jockeyed for position, rumbling onto the perimeter road. Although the crews had been warned for ops on Christmas Day, mercifully they were stood down shortly afterwards. Now the Main Force was rejoining the battle, off to turn again the rubble of the Big City.

The last few days were a blur and Suzy was worn out, confused. She was afraid she had made a terrible mistake that she was going to regret for the rest of her life. The trouble was she did not know what she had done, or why she should feel this way. Her heart had leapt when Peter told her he had been ordered to take three days leave and that he would be spending it at Waltham Grange as a guest of the Mess. Naively, she had imagined that they would see a great deal of each other, the best of mutual Christmas presents. However, the RAF had had other plans. Even though there were no ops, her duties on the operations section kept her busy during the day and in the evenings she found herself competing with Peter's numerous cronies. She had seen relatively little of him, hardly had him to herself at all and when they contrived to be alone together, things had been strained. Not overtly, it was worse than that. Things were just left unsaid, unmentioned. It was as if they had had their fling, got away with it, and decided to defer to the reality of their situation. Reunited, they had initially forgotten their inhibitions and been themselves, their old selves. Saying goodnight outside the Waafery after dancing the night away in the Mess they had kissed as lovers; but in the morning they were strangers, again.

Peter had gone flying, regardless of the weather. For the joy of it, he said. She resented it, bitterly. He might as well have not been on leave. In the evenings she was weary from a day in the Ops Room, he would be alive, exhilarated from joyriding in a Lancaster at a hundred feet over Lincolnshire. They met for a drink in the Mess, walked across the wintery airfield, made desultory conversation. Sometimes they held hands, often they walked apart, avoiding contact. Silences came between them. One evening they had driven into Lincoln in a borrowed car. Because it was Christmas everything was shut up, nobody was about but at least they were alone, separate from the station and the Lancasters.

Something had gone wrong. Peter seemed different, distant. He was as kind, solicitous, gentle as he had always been but sometimes he was...elsewhere, even when she was in his arms. She wondered if it was her, if she had grown up too quickly and not realised it.

Had they really changed so much?

She did not believe it.

Underneath they were the same. They felt the same feelings for each other. Yet while they had talked of many things, it was exclusively of small things. For example, there was no more talk of stealing away to Lincoln, nor happy reminiscences of their clumsy, glorious love-making in that creaky, rickety old bed. Simply a shared relief that the event had had no unforeseen, awkward consequences.

The first Lancaster was rolling.

Around Suzy the sightseers and well-wishers cheered lustily. No ops for nearly a week got on everybody's nerves, Christmas or not. The Main Force was returning to Berlin. Tonight there would be over 700 hundred heavies in the air. Flight-Lieutenant Ramsey, the Operations Officer, had visibly perked when he heard the news the Halifax Force was rejoining the battle. The fighters always went for the Halifaxes first.

The last Berlin raid on Christmas Eve had been a dismal failure. The Pathfinders had randomly unloaded Sky Markers and TIs across the south-easterly districts of the city and a broad tract of open countryside south of the city. Subsequently, a large number of aircraft had bombed many, many miles outside the city boundaries. The rest of the bombing had probably been scattered across the suburbs of Kopenick and Treptow. The raid was a fiasco – albeit a relatively minor fiasco by the standards of the age - mitigated only by the fact that the Luftwaffe had failed to seriously inconvenience the bomber stream and *only* 16 Lancasters had been lost.

All 14 Lancasters despatched from Waltham Grange had returned safe and sound, bar one aircraft which had landed minus its bomb-aimer. C-Charlie had had a brush with a fighter over

Berlin and it seemed the poor boy had panicked, baled out. It happened from time to time. It had happened at least twice while Suzy was at Ansham Wolds.

'So and so baled out without permission due to temporary insanity...' Usually accounted for the matter in the Squadron Operations Record Book. That or something along the lines of: *'So and so evidently misheard the order to abandon the aircraft...'*

"It might snow tomorrow," somebody said in the crowd behind her. "It's cold enough."

"I hope not!" A man objected. "The Groupie will have us out on the runways with shovels! Bugger that for a laugh!"

"Naw, don't be dense!" Another voice offered, irritably. "If there's snow they'll be a stand down. You'll see!"

"Don't you believe it, mate!"

L-London, Clive Irving's aircraft, lurched up to the threshold, ran up its Merlins. Behind the Lancaster, more aircraft queued for the off. There was just enough light to make out the 'ops eggs', bomb symbols, painted below the cockpit on the port fuselage. L-London, Irving's faithful stead, was an old warhorse with 24 ops under her belt.

L-London surged forward.

Suzy was thinking about Peter.

About now, thirty miles away, his aircraft would be lining up for takeoff at Ansham Wolds. He would be flying tonight. His crew would be back from leave and Jack Gordon fit to fight his weight. There would have been a queue of unattached, 'floating' aircrew eager to fill dead Tom Dennison's shoes and Peter would be keen to give 'the chaps' an early outing to erase the bad memories of their last op.

"Good luck, my darling," Suzy said silently.

Chapter 30

Wednesday 29th December, 1943
Lancaster R-Robert, 20 miles SSW of Hanover

Jack Gordon adjusted his oxygen mask. There was ice on the inside of the fuselage, ice on the wings and R-Robert was climbing sluggishly above an endless sea of cloud. The night was black, evil and deadly about them. The cold seeped into his bones finding out every weak spot, every newly healed wound, every scar and crack.

Nancy had implored, nagged, and berated him for going back so soon.

'Oh, Jack. You know you're still not right!'

He had gritted his teeth, girded his courage.

'Look, I don't want to risk getting left behind. You know, having to finish the tour with strangers.'

'Peter wouldn't let that happen!' Nancy had objected, vehemently. 'And you know it, *Jack Gordon*!'

The 'Jack Gordon' tended to come out just before Nancy lost her temper. It was a warning sign not to be lightly ignored. There was nothing demure about Nancy when she came to the boil. Notwithstanding this incendiary trait, he loved her dearly. They sparked off each other. If they were going to have their share of stormy interludes; they were also going to have an outrageous amount of fun making up afterwards.

"Navigator to pilot," he called, flicking the intercom switch. It was time to exercise a little sang-froid. "I'm in the astrodome, now. Don't even think about taking evasive action until I'm out of here. Don't you bloody dare!"

"Scout's honour, Jack!" Tilliard drawled with the apparent assurance of a man who had not a worry in the world. "If we bump into a fighter I'll just let it shoot us down, old man."

"You do that!" The Australian retorted.

R-Robert steadied, stopped weaving.

Jack got down to business immediately, sighting his sextant on the Pole Star. Without a ground fix since taking off from Ansham Wolds and relying purely on dead reckoning, they could easily be fifty miles off track. He had calculated their position as being mid-way between Hanover and Bielefeld, pretty much on the nail, but only a fool trusted dead reckoning when the stars were out. There were no fools onboard R-Robert. He tried to slow himself down, fought the urge to hurry. He needed a good star sight, a couple if possible.

"Pilot to navigator. How much longer, Jack?"

"Minute or two, Skipper!"

"Roger."

The gunners had reported combats over Holland, heavies falling into the clouds. Since then things had gone quiet. An optimist might hope the fighters had lost contact with the bomber stream: a pessimist would assume the fighters were lurking up ahead, waiting to pounce. Jack was a pessimist. He scrawled figures on his pad, lifted the sextant to his eye, checked the previous angle.

"Navigator to pilot. Finished up here, Skipper!"

Tilliard instantly banked the Lancaster to port, off the straight and level.

Jack clambered through the curtain, slumped

into his chair, turned on the angle-poise lamp over his cluttered desk and plugged in his intercom. Swiftly plotting the star sights on his charts, he recalculated R-Robert's position, and compared it with his dead reckoning log.

He flicked his intercom switch.

"Navigator to pilot. We're more or less on track but a bit behind on time. Can we increase IAS by ten knots and come right five degrees to one-one-oh for five minutes."

The pilot acknowledged the changes without comment, echoed them in confirmation. The Merlins quickened and the compass repeater showed the small change of course. Jack settled, turned his mind to re-fixing the wind speeds. Out came the slide rule. He retraced the route back to the Dutch coast. Presently, he scribbled his results on a scrap of paper and pushed it through the blackout curtain separating him from Tom Dennison's replacement as W/T operator, a small, hard-eyed man.

Flight Sergeant George Simpson took the note, made a thumbs up signal to his navigator and readjusted the curtain. The new man in the crew was three trips into his second tour. His first had concluded over Essen in January. Between tours he had been posted to Lindholme and had had no qualms employing the Lindholme connection to jump the queue of floaters and odd sods competing to catch Squadron Leader Tilliard's eye.

"Yes," the Skipper had grinned, when he introduced himself. "I thought you looked familiar. George, isn't it?"

"I flew with Mister Irving, sir. Mostly."

"Of course you did. I should imagine you know your stuff?"

"Yes, sir. Thank you for saying so, sir."

And that was that!

"Jolly good. I'll introduce you to the chaps, George."

Simpson made a point of never looking outside the aircraft during an operation. Some crews liked their W/T op to take turns as a lookout in the cockpit. Not this crew. In this crew the pilot flew the aircraft, the gunners kept watch, the engineer too when he had time, the bomb-aimer *Windowed*, the navigator navigated and the W/T Op 'played' the frequencies. Everybody knew exactly what their job was and everybody knew that job inside out; he devoted his whole attention to his equipment and left the looking outside to the others. His job was to man the radio and to manipulate the various associated devices piled high on the desk in front of him. This was a proper crew: nobody messed about and *everybody* pulled his weight.

The day he joined the crew the Skipper had taken him to see the Wingco's W/T Op, Bert Pound, and asked Bert - man to man, none of the normal officer and gentleman bull, respectfully and politely, like he was asking Bert a huge personal favour - if he would 'brief George on the best way to play the frequencies'. Bert Pound was a mine of information, ten times more genned up than the Communications Officer or any of his allegedly 'expert' non-flying flunkies.

George Simpson felt as if he had come home.

When Jack Gordon interrupted him he had been employing the tried and tested techniques he had learned from the Wingco's W/T Op to trawl the German night fighter frequencies, attempting to pick up Luftwaffe radio traffic. Every heavy had a transmitter mounted inside one of its engine nacelles. R-Robert's was fixed in the port-inner. The idea was to listen out for German chit chat, then broadcast the wrath of the Merlin at full volume over the same frequency. Tonight, to his chagrin there was nothing worth jamming. All he was getting was static and faint, faraway, indecipherably fragmented traffic.

Simpson stopped what he was doing, retuned the set and swiftly, deftly dashed off Jack Gordon's 'found wind'. God in Heaven it was a relief to be flying again with chaps who really knew what they were doing! Flying with sprogs or in scratch crews, was a mug's game. The single blot on the horizon was that sooner or later the Skipper would run a cursory eye over his sickness chits. The skipper was the sort of diligent, detail hungry chap who made a point of reading *all* the paperwork. When he eventually got around to reading his file he was going to discover his W/T Op had sat out half-a-dozen ops with neuralgia, or influenza, or a mysteriously sprained ankle, and once even persuaded the dentist to extract a perfectly healthy tooth so as to avoid having to fly that night with a particularly inept sprog crew. Until Tom Dennison had bought it, things were looking bad. He had reached the point where the next logical step was to get himself arrested. A trip into Lincoln to pick a fight with the first Aussie he met, or maybe a brick through somebody's window, anything to get himself locked up. He was not a coward. But why should he die for nothing? He had been a sprog once, survived somehow and vowed 'never again'.

He told himself to concentrate on the frequencies. Within five minutes he picked up a snatch of German. He tuned carefully, precisely for about a minute. Bert Pound said it was always worth listening to the controllers chat, to jot down any new code words, phrases or departures from normal operating procedures. The chit chat might not mean much to him but perhaps the intelligence people might make something of it. Nothing new tonight, so after a while - with no little glee - he transmitted the hellish din of R-Robert's port inner Merlin over the selected frequency at maximum power.

"Talk over that, Fritz!" He muttered to himself.

George Simpson was from the East End of London. His family had been bombed out in 1940, an aunt and an uncle killed, and the community in which he had grown up wiped off the face of the earth in a single night. George Simpson did not like Germans and had never made bones about the fact he had volunteered for flying duties specifically to kill Germans. The violence of his anger and his lust for vengeance had cooled a degree or two in the intervening years, but in George Simpson's book anything and everything on the ground in Germany was fair game.

The Skipper was calling round the crew stations. Squadron Leader Tilliard called around every few minutes to make sure everybody was awake. Nobody else used the intercom unless they had something to report, excepting the Navigator, and even he kept the banter short and sweet.

Tilliard's crew were really on the ball. With a crew like this a man had both a fighting chance of getting through a tour and a gold-plated opportunity to kill a lot of Germans.

"Pilot to W/T op."

"W/T op to pilot. Hearing you loud and clear, Skipper!"

"Good man."

Chapter 31

Thursday 30th December, 1943
RAF Ansham Wolds, Lincolnshire

Stalemate. Bloody stalemate. Once again the Big City had been shielded by clouds. The good news was that the chop rate was on the low side: only 20 heavies, not one of them from Ansham Wolds. The bad news was that although hundreds of bomb loads had been dropped, most of them had been scattered across rural northern Germany.

In the morning Adam found Group Captain Alexander somewhat under the weather and in an uncharacteristically subdued mood.

"I think it's time we had a chat," the older man said, waving his Squadron Commander to take a seat. He sneezed, dusted his face with a big chequered handkerchief and paused to regain his wind.

"Oh. About anything in particular, sir?"

The Station Master and the Deputy AOC had gone into conclave at the Prof's funeral and he could guess what they had been taking about. *Him.* He had been at Ansham Wolds three months. Including his time at Waltham Grange he had been continuously in command of a front-line squadron for well over six. That was long enough and if he was honest about it, he did not need to be told he was overdue a rest.

"This and that."

"I see."

"I'm sure you do," smiled the older man.

Adam caught his mood, chuckled ruefully.

"I'm in no hurry to fly a desk, sir."

"No, of course not." Alexander leaned back in his chair. Notwithstanding his cold and his wheezing lungs he began to pack his pipe. At his back flecks of snow fell on the cold ground outside the window. Condensation dripped off the clammy end wall of the Nissen hut. "I gather Mac's still got his heart set on Pathfinders?"

"Yes, sir. He's already withdrawn one request. It wouldn't be right to ask him to withdraw a second." In fact Adam had given his word to Mac that if he presented another request in the New Year, he would endorse it.

"Fair enough. Group have been asked, informally you understand, not to block requests for transfer to Eight Group."

"It doesn't surprise me, sir."

Alexander nodded solemnly.

"The Pathfinders have had a pretty rough ride lately. Lost too many good men. If things don't get any better, the Deputy AOC thinks we might have to start nominating experienced crews for transfer. Be the thin end of the wedge, of course. But there you go."

Adam tapped a cigarette on the back of his hand, lit up. Nothing alarmed him so much as the continuing decline in the performance of the Pathfinders. Personally, he would much rather that the Pathfinders were stiffened with old lags at the expense of the Main Force than have attacks continually going off half-cock, or worse, like last night.

"Something's got to be done, sir."

"Quite," agreed the Old Man. "It's always baffled me why you've never put in for Pathfinders yourself?"

This took Adam unawares. He had learned his trade in 5 Group and in 5 Group it had often seemed as if 8 Group, rather than the Luftwaffe was the real enemy. Honestly and truly it had never crossed his mind to opt for Pathfinders.

"Not that I'm complaining," Alexander went on. "I think we're a good team. You and I. A damned good team, what!"

"Er, yes, sir."

"Who do you see filling Mac's shoes?"

"Henry Barlow."

"Mac's old lags won't like that. Taking orders from a B Flighter?"

Adam knew the Old Man was teasing him.

"Henry's well thought of, sir."

"Yes. I know. He's the obvious choice. I just hope Peter Tilliard doesn't take it into his head to follow Mac's lead."

Adam shook his head.

"I think Peter's a Main Force man, sir."

Group Captain Alexander grunted. He had not intended to fence. He had resolved to take the bull by the horns, to say what he had to say and to clear the air. Belatedly, he summoned his resolve.

"The AOC has decided that you need a rest, my boy," he declared, feeling embarrassed, and somehow in the wrong. "Bob Nicholson is to take command of the Squadron before the end of January. I have recommended that all things being equal, Bob should take over in about three weeks from now. That'll give him a chance to get a few more ops under his belt. I think that's important if he's going to command the chaps' respect."

Adam nodded silently. His eleven ops at Ansham Wolds had raised his personal tally to seventy-eight. A good innings.

"I don't propose to inform Bob until a little nearer the time," Alexander continued, mightily relieved to have got it off his chest. "But I felt it was only right and proper to fill you in. So you know the lie of the land, as it were."

"Thank you, sir. I appreciate it."

Adam collected Rufus from his office and stalked out across the frosty airfield. As he walked, his thoughts ranged back over the years to the Wilhelmshaven raid. The events of that afternoon four years ago were never far away, a constant reminder that disaster lurked behind the next cloud. Wilhelmshaven had been the first of his seventy-eight 'official' bomber ops - he had actually flown twenty others, a mixture of leaflet dropping, 'nickeling', trips, and missions as an observer or passenger, sometimes legitimately, others not - and afterwards he had always known he was living on borrowed time. That his life was no longer his own, forfeit.

The sonorous drone of an approaching Lancaster intruded on his brooding. He looked up to see the bomber swoop in low over the perimeter fence, settle on the icy tarmac. It ran into the distance, slowing, slowing. The Squadron was expecting delivery of three new aircraft and he assumed this Lancaster was the first of the batch. Visibility over the high wold was poor, low cloud and snow squalls had grounded his crews but nothing deterred the fearless women of the ATS.

He watched the new arrival taxiing in the misty distance. Ansham Wolds was at its desolate, bleak, forsaken best. The vast, open expanse of the airfield was virtually empty and the faraway, muted thunder of the lone Lancaster's Merlins drifted fitfully on the breeze. How odd was it that here where a man could not help but confront his despair; he had faced down so many of his demons and found a strange kind of peace?

"I say!" Called out a familiar, well-intentioned, apologetic voice. "I say, Wing-Commander. I'm dreadfully sorry to bother you, but could I have a word?"

Adam half-turned, and eyed the breathless figure of the Reverend Poore. Although he liked to think he was as approachable as the next man, he was savvy enough to recognise that the majority of his aircrew were young, impressionable and by and large, middlingly terrified of him. Only a handful of men, Mac, Peter Tilliard, Henry Barlow and one or two of his old lags were sufficiently unafraid of him to trust him with a confidence, let alone to speak freely in his presence. The Padre, on the other hand, enjoyed a privileged status. He was an outsider, a free agent, and to his credit he took full advantage of his position.

"Of course, Padre. What can I do for you?"

It transpired that the Reverend Poore wanted to speak to him about the case of an A Flight gunner whose father had been taken ill. The boy was torn between the Squadron and his family, worried that if he applied for compassionate leave his crew would leave him behind and he would have to start his tour again with strangers.

"Flight Commander's discretion. Have a word with Mac," Adam advised the Padre. "I'm sure he'll know what to do."

The Reverend Poore nodded, happy to settle for this. He had discovered early in his tenure at Ansham Wolds that the Wingco never went over the heads of his Flight Commanders. However, it never did any harm for him to mention that he'd 'mentioned' this, or that case, 'to the CO'. Some said the CO liked to give a chap enough rope to hang himself with; but it was his observation that when the CO gave a man a little slack to play with, it was more for when the going got tough.

"Yes, sir."

Adam suspected the Padre had a list of other matters to bring to his attention. Invariably, his opening gambit was something safe, easily dispensed, and thornier matters followed in due course. The Padre was a model of tact in these things, a man with a subtle mind, patient and quietly tenacious in his work.

"God, it's beautiful out here, don't you think?"

"Lonely. And yes, beautiful, too."

Adam looked past the cleric's shoulder, avoided his eye.

"How's the atonement going, Padre?" He inquired, recalling their first conversation. It was asked sincerely, without a hint of frivolity and the older man took it onboard in same spirit.

"Apace, sir."

Adam began to saunter towards the faraway watchtower with Rufus trotting close at his heels.

"I think the chaps are holding up their end," he

remarked. "Don't you?"

The older man nodded, intently. The courage and the fortitude of the crews had humbled the Padre from the outset, reminded him of the stoicism of the men he had fought with in Flanders.

"More than holding up their end, I'd say."

"Yes," murmured the younger man. "Of course, the real test will be what happens in the next month or so." They walked on, each man a little lost in his thoughts. "Do you remember our first tete-a-tete, Padre?"

"As if it was yesterday, sir."

It was no lie. The events of that day were deeply, indelibly etched in the Reverend Poore's consciousness. The Wingco's genuine friendliness in the Operations Room, their breakneck drive across the airfield, the directness of his words. Then later that awful flight test, the dreadful nausea, the humiliation of vomiting on himself, closely followed by the elation that came from being accepted for what he was in this strange, unnatural place miles from anywhere. To the crews he was the 'puking Padre', the old fogey who had concealed his vertigo from the Wingco and in so doing glimpsed something of the terrors aircrew took for granted. The brotherhood of the crews was a tight-knit, secretive order and the mysteries of that order might have been closed to him forever but for the insights he had gained that day, and subsequently, through the friendship of the charismatic and quite extraordinary young man – barely half his age - who commanded 647 Squadron.

"Do you remember," Adam went on, quietly, "what I said about most of the chaps not making it through the winter?"

The Padre nodded. "Yes, sir." It was not the sort of thing a man quickly forgot.

"Keep it under your hat, but the odds are I shall be screened fairly soon. This is my third tour. The rules are a bit vague, but I've done more than twenty odd ops since June and that's about par for the course. That means I won't be seeing this thing through. It's good you get on so well with Bob Nicholson because I'm afraid the worst may still be to come. He's going to need all the help he can get."

The Reverend Poore was silent. Try as he might he could not imagine Ansham Wolds without Adam Chantrey.

Chapter 32

Thursday 30th December, 1943
The Gatekeeper's Lodge, Ansham Wolds, Lincolnshire

Eleanor had laid a place at the table for Adam. Not because she took his presence for granted. More as a statement of her belief in the future.

If he could come tonight, he would.

There had been very little flying that afternoon. Only a handful of aircraft had actually flown over Ansham Wolds. Empty skies by day meant no ops by night and besides, a thin carpet of snow lay across the Wold. Winter had clamped down over Lincolnshire. So she laid a place at the kitchen table for the man, settled Jonathan and Emily in their chairs, busied herself with the pots and pans on the range. The scent of wood smoke filled the kitchen. Hearing the car in the lane, the squeaking of brakes, the firm knock at the front door Eleanor clung onto her composure.

"Johnny, would you answer the door, please." The boy ran out of the room. There were voices in the parlour: Adam promising her son that tomorrow he would be able to build a snowman, Jonathan asking him if he would help him build it.

"If I can," the man replied. "But no promises."

Eleanor smiled at Adam. He kissed her cheek, took his seat.

"Now, now, Johnny," she half-soothed, half-chided. "You know Uncle Adam is very busy. He has the whole Squadron to think of. Not just us.

He can't just drop everything. Not even to build a snowman."

Adam laughed, patted the boy's head.

"I wish I could. I remember the first snowman I built. I was about your age, Johnny. The sun shone the next day and it melted. I was inconsolable. Of course the place to go to build the best snowmen is the mountains. Trouble is we don't have too many real mountains in this country. Ben Nevis, a few other hills in Scotland, Snowdon in Wales, I suppose. But they're not real mountains. Not mountains like you see in the Alps. Not like the ones in southern Germany, in Bavaria. The mountains there are so tall you get a crick in your neck just looking at them. In the Alps some of the mountains are covered in snow all year around, not just in the winter."

Eleanor ladled mutton stew onto the plates. Small helpings for the children and herself, trencherman's ration's for Adam even though she knew his appetite was often slight. She thought a man should carry a little spare flesh to keep him warm in the cold of the night. Knowing full well that he was too polite to protest about the size of his portion, and always did his best to eat the better part of whatever she put in front of him she took an innocent pleasure in piling his plate high. She put fresh baked bread on the table to mop up the meat juices. The family tucked in.

"A good day at the office, darling?" Eleanor inquired, presently.

Adam looked up, met her eye. He was proud of her. No matter what her inner turmoil or the millstone of grief that weighed upon her she was determined to hide it from the children.

"The chaps are all accounted for," he told her, conversationally.

"Good," she murmured. "Do you think we'll get any more snow tomorrow?"

"I hope so. The chaps deserve a proper party. Tomorrow being New Year's Eve, and so forth."

"That was my next question," Eleanor returned, brightly. "How does the RAF celebrate the New Year?"

"With a proper party," he grinned.

"Silly question. Do you remember what you were doing this time last year?" She asked, fondly, unsuspectingly.

Adam shrugged, uneasily. The question awakened memories better left dormant. The words of Helen Fulshawe's three month old letter suddenly filled his thoughts. Attempting to veil his discomfort he winked at Emmy. The girl screwed up her face, giggled.

"I was on leave," he recollected evenly, despite his churning emotions. "Staying with Bert and Helen Fulshawe. Down in Gloucestershire. I'd left Kelmington the week before, been down to Tavistock to see Henrietta, my sister and her brood for Christmas. I was on my way to High Wycombe to serve my penance on the Chief's Staff. It seems like an awfully long time ago. Almost another lifetime."

"This will be our fourth New Year in Ansham Wolds," Eleanor returned, a little wistfully. "I wonder where we will all be this time next year?"

"Where indeed?"

"A year's a long time," Eleanor declared. "By

then the war might be over. Everything might be different?"

"Perhaps."

The conversation became stilted. The children exchanged looks, uncertain what to make of their elders' distraction. Adam was thinking about Bert Fulshawe, his unquenchable optimism and his love of life. And the lingering unquiet feelings that he harboured even now for his dead friend's widow. Bert was dead and buried; his feelings for Helen were not. Nor would they ever be while he continued to live a lie. Eleanor, realising something was wrong, tried very hard not to broadcast her concern.

"Sorry," he muttered, when the dishes were being cleared away. "I'm supposed to be cheering you up. I'm not doing a very good job, am I?"

Eleanor greeted this with a smile.

"Don't be silly, darling. I don't know what I'd have done without you these last few weeks. I really don't." She touched his hand. "You've been an angel. My guardian angel."

He rose from the table; if he was an angel, he had long ago fallen from grace.

"If you don't mind I'll step outside. A little fresh air might help clear my head."

"Go ahead. Don't stay out too long, you'll catch your death."

He stepped into the darkened garden. Large, wispy snowflakes floated in the air, and lay like a cloak on the ground. It was bitterly cold but he was oblivious to it. He pulled out a cigarette, lit up. Inside the kitchen he listened to Eleanor moving around, the muted clatter of pots, pans, dishes and cutlery. He ran his fingertips over Helen's cigarette case. The metal was clammy, chilly to his touch. It was more than a year since he had last held Helen in his arms: two squadrons ago, twenty-two ops ago and god only knew how many letters to next of kin ago.

'Bert's had a jolly good war,' Helen had said, bitterly. 'I've had you. A fair exchange. But then you've had it both ways, haven't you? You've had a bloody good war and you've had me!' He and Helen had quarrelled from the start, but more often and for less reason with the passage of time. Helen had never understood that however much a chap pretended that the ghastliness of ops was water off a duck's back, underneath fresh scar tissue formed each day. Adam's war had gone sour at Kelmington. The death of the old 380 Squadron and with it, the death of his 'Boscombe Flight' had signalled the end of his 'good war'. His war had stopped being a great adventure at Kelmington, and become instead a waking nightmare. One after another the battle had consumed his friends and in the end it had very nearly broken him. The break with Helen had been the last straw. The bombshell struck him within days of his screening, before he had had a chance to come to terms with the nightmare. Kelmington had knocked the stuffing out of him. So much so that for a while he was, more or less, content marking time on the Chief's Staff at High Wycombe.

Returning to ops he had made a new start, thrown himself into his duties, almost succeeded in shutting out the past until fate had played one last, cruel card; sending him to Ansham Wolds and forcing him to confront the great lie of his life. Now it was time to stop running, to put an end to the lies.

"Come in out of the cold, darling," Eleanor prompted from the open doorway. The weak light from the kitchen spilled into the garden, across the snowy ground. "Or at least put your coat on."

"I'll come in."

The woman brushed flakes of snow off his shoulders. Wordlessly, she looked him up and down.

"Sorry. Things on my mind."

"I guessed that," Eleanor chided him, mildly. "Half-way through dinner you went all misty-eyed and faraway. You only do that when you're worried about something. *Really worried*, that is."

"Is it that obvious?"

She nodded.

"Will you tell me about it?"

"Yes. Everything," he promised.

Chapter 33

Thursday 30th December, 1943
The Hare and Hounds, Kingston Magna, Lincolnshire

C Flight was in residence. The ancient oaken timbers of the tavern shook to the roar of a score of lusty voices raised in song. Cloudy wreaths of cigarette smoke hung thickly in the air, the fire blazed in the hearth and despite the coldness of the night it was hot and sticky in the low-beamed bar.

Unusually, Jack Gordon was not leading the singing, and stranger still, mid-way through the evening he remained more or less sober. He slipped out of the door of the snug, and sought the quiet of the snowy night as the strains of a familiar chorus drifted to his ears.

"*Oh, they say there's a Lancaster leaving Berlin! She's, bound for fair Blighty's shore! Laden with seven terrified sprogs! Flying back to the girls they adore!*"

Normally, he would have shouted it to the rafters with a fine disregard for tunefulness. Tonight, he was subdued, unable to join in the celebrations. He kept thinking about Tom Dennison. Most of the chaps doing the singing were newcomers to the Squadron, not yet in the picture. Last night he had awoken in a cold sweat, imagined his perspiration was Tom's blood: warm, fresh, clotting blood dripping off his brow, and soaking into his sheets. You could wash a man's blood off your hands but it was much harder to wash it out of your head.

Black Thursday had been his forty-fourth op, every one of them on Lancasters, most of them to Germany. It was a bit late in the day to be getting twitchy.

"They say there's a Lancaster leaving Leipzig!"

Jack smoked his cigarette.

"Ah, there you are, old man!" Peter Tilliard announced, approaching his friend.

"No ops tomorrow if this keeps up," Jack Gordon said, waving at the falling snow, effecting disinterest.

Tilliard shrugged, sniffed.

"Dashed stuffy in there," he remarked, idly.

"Oh, they say there's a Lancaster leaving the Ruhr! She's, bound for fair Blighty's shore!"

"The chaps are in good voice," Jack returned. "For Poms, that is."

The other man laughed, slapped the Australian's shoulder. Peter Tilliard had observed the change in his navigator in recent days. The business with Tom Dennison was at the root of it. That and Nancy Bowman. His friend had taken Tom's death badly. He had paused, dared to think things through, dared to confront the logic of their situation. He knew from his own recent experience it was always a mistake to stop and think.

"Oh, they say there's a Lancaster leaving Cologne! She's, bound for fair Blighty's shore! Laden with seven terrified sprogs!"

"I hate this bloody song!" Jack declared, softly, bitterly.

Tilliard shoved his hands into his pockets, stamped his feet to ward off the cold and waited for Jack to continue. His friend had things on his mind, things best said. Once said they could be put to one side, cleaned out of his system. Hopefully, then he would be more his old self.

"I hate it all," Jack went on.

"Rubbish!" Tilliard objected, half-hoping it would somehow break the dark cycle of his friend's thoughts. "You're half way through a tour. About to get hitched. You're just a bit broody, that's all!"

"Oh, they say there's a Lancaster leaving Essen! She's, bound for fair Blighty's shore! Laden with seven terrified sprogs! Flying back to the girls they adore!"

"Maybe."

"Got a lot on your mind, that's all."

Jack half-turned, looked at Peter Tilliard.

"I've been at this game nearly four years, now," he said, wearily. "I used to write to my folks and tell them that we only bombed military targets. Not like the Jerries. Well, I'm still waiting to bomb something military, Peter."

"Military, industrial, civilian? What does it matter? It all amounts to the same thing, doesn't it?"

Jack chuckled softly.

"Maybe, that's the trouble."

"I think it's high time you went back inside and sank a few more pints!" Tilliard decided, realising there was little profit in further debate. "If Nancy sees you sober she'll only worry. You mustn't go worrying her unnecessarily. Not with her in her condition."

"Suppose not."

"That's the ticket!"

"Oh, they say there's a Lancaster leaving

Stuttgart! She's, bound for fair Blighty's shore! Laden with seven terrified sprogs! Flying back to the girls they adore!"

"Where did you go?" Nancy demanded, perching precariously on Jack's knee amidst the crush of bodies, almost shouting into his ear above the crescendo of raised voices.

"I needed a bit of fresh air, my lovely!" He yelled.

"You could have come out the back with me!"

He grinned roguishly.

"Isn't that how we got into all this trouble in the first place?"

Nancy flashed her eyes at him, giggled.

"You're terrible man, Jack Gordon!"

"Oh, they say there's a Lancaster leaving Frankfurt! She's, bound for fair Blighty's shore! Laden with seven terrified sprogs! Flying back to the girls they adore!"

Peter Tilliard leaned on the bar and bawled out the chorus. He viewed the lovers from afar, half of him envying them, the other half relieved that he had only himself to worry about, now. Seeing Suzy again had clarified many things and forced him to face up to reality.

He sipped his beer.

"Oh, they say there's a Lancaster leaving Dortmund!"

All around him *his* crews drank, sang, laughed. A few men had WAAF girlfriends hanging on their arms, most were huddled with their comrades, the band of brothers with whom they had chosen to fight and with whom they would almost certainly die. But that was in the future. Tonight they were alive, shutting out all knowledge of the many forms of death that rode with them to the distant cities. Tonight, they were celebrating their survival, not dwelling on their mortality.

"Oh, they say there's a Lancaster leaving Kassel! She's, bound for fair Blighty's shore!"

Tilliard edged into a corner. Suzy's face was always in his thoughts but whenever he weakened he reminded himself that since his arrival at Ansham Wolds in August, no crew had completed a tour. Several crews had transferred to Pathfinders in mid-tour, one well on the way to the magic figure of thirty ops, but nobody had actually survived a tour. End of tour parties were a distant memory on 647 Squadron. A thing of legend, deeply shrouded in aircrew mythology.

"Oh, they say there's a Lancaster leaving Hamburg! She's, bound for fair Blighty's shore! Laden with seven terrified sprogs!"

They were living in a strange, unnatural twilight between life and death. A wise man paid the ferryman the day he joined his Squadron, booked his passage across the Styx well in advance and made his peace with his maker. Death came in too many ways over Germany and sooner or later the odds caught up with the luckiest of men. On Civvy street he would have been down on bended knee begging Suzy to marry him. Civvy street was a million miles away. The war was not about to suddenly end, for all he knew it might go on for years and a month was an eternity on the squadrons. If he was a cat he would have already used up his nine lives. A fortnight ago he had been stooging around in the fog with the gauges reading

EMPTY. By rights they ought to have bought it then. Then and there. Now more than ever he was living on borrowed time.

"Oh, they say there's a Lancaster leaving Berlin! She's, bound for fair Blighty's shore! Laden with seven terrified sprogs! Flying back to the girls they adore!"

It was better to hurt Suzy a little now than to be the cause of untold pain later. She was a sensible girl; hopefully she would understand that he was thinking of her, trying to protect her. More likely, she would despise him. And rightly so.

Chapter 34

Thursday 30th December, 1943
The Gatekeeper's Lodge, Ansham Wolds, Lincolnshire

Together they stared into the fire. In the warm quietness of the parlour they were alone with their thoughts as the evening drew on and the clock ticked towards nine.

Eleanor had allowed the children to linger downstairs past their normal bed time. Her son and daughter had accepted Adam into their lives with a lingering shyness as a benign, benevolent uncle. Johnny's eyes lit up when Adam had told him his elder brother, Paul, was a Spitfire pilot in the Battle of Britain.

'Did he shoot down lots of Germans?'

'Rather,' Adam replied, ruefully, winking at Eleanor. 'I should say. Paul was a frightfully brave chap.'

The boy frowned, forewarned perhaps by the man's tone.

'Is he dead?'

Adam nodded.

'Yes. A long time ago.'

'Is he in Heaven with my daddy?'

Eleanor opened her mouth to speak. She meant to say something soothing, and to direct the talk onto safer, less rocky pastures.

Adam spoke first. 'I should think so.'

As the man and the woman stared into the fire they talked about nothing in particular for some minutes, as if to be certain that the children were in their beds, fast asleep. Then, Eleanor attempted to draw him out.

"You've never talked about your brother?"

Adam glanced to her, then back to the fire.

"No. We never really got on, I'm afraid."

"Oh, I see."

"He was five years older and I was always getting under his feet. Father would always take his side, mother would take mine. Paul was everything I wanted to be. Things came easily to him. I could never catch him up, no matter how hard I tried."

Eleanor clasped her hands on her lap, viewed him fondly. She did not speak. Adam needed no more prompting than to know that she was listening, waiting to hear more.

"You'd have liked Paul," he went on, wryly. "Everybody liked Paul. A man's man, if you know what I mean. Bit like Bert Fulshawe, actually. Broken out of the same kind of mold. Paul was one of the chaps who used to do the dare-Devil spins and rolls at Hendon before the war. He used to love that, thrilling the crowds and being at the centre of things. He said mixing it with the Luftwaffe over Kent was just like Hendon, except that it was on a bigger stage and everybody was using live ammo. That was Paul all over, pretending it was some great big game. He was on Hurricanes when the balloon went up. His squadron went over to France with the B.E.F. He was shot down twice. Luckily, over friendly territory. In the end he got out by the skin of his teeth. You know, literally taking off between the panzers with bullets flying everywhere.

Back in England he was posted to Spitfires and when the party got going in August 1940 he was pretty much in the thick of things. A couple of weeks before he was killed he got his own Squadron."

The timbre of the man's voice betrayed him. A great deal remained unspoken, concealed. Eleanor wondered why. Families could be very odd, her own was an object lesson; riven by its differences and yet, when it mattered most, united in its darkest hours.

"I used to think Paul and Bert Fulshawe were more like brothers than Paul and I," Adam recollected. "Bert never said, but I should imagine it was Paul who asked him to take me under his wing. I suppose Bert was the big brother I'd never had. I think that's the worst of it."

"I don't understand?" Eleanor returned, confused. "The worst of what, darling?"

"It's a long story."

"Tell me anyway."

Adam steeled himself.

"I thought I'd put it all behind me," he explained, lowly. "Really, I did. But then they sent me up here, I met you, and in a funny sort of way, things have come full circle."

Eleanor suppressed a tremor of anxiety, remained silent.

Adam paused, organised his thoughts.

"The last time I met Paul it was in London the night before he went down to take command at Malling Hall," he explained. "That was in early September 1940. He introduced me to his fiancée, Mary. Things were a bit strained over dinner. I put it down to Paul being under the weather, worrying about the new Squadron, and so forth. After dinner Paul suggested we stretch our legs, get a breath of fresh air. As soon as we were outside he flew at me, gave me a frightful dressing down. In the street, in front of passersby. He wasn't a chap to beat about the bush, not when his dander was up. He told me I was a disgrace and that it was high time I mended my ways. That so far as he was concerned, until I did the decent thing, he and I were no longer brothers. No longer 'connected'. He said I was no longer welcome in his house. *Persona non grata*, as it were. We very nearly came to blows. We probably would have if Mary hadn't heard our raised voices and come out to see what the fuss was. I didn't bother to pick up my kit, I just left, walked away, spent the night in a hotel and in the morning I went back to my Squadron. It was the last time I saw Paul alive. He was killed in action twelve days later. Mary wouldn't speak to me at his funeral."

"Surely, she didn't blame you for Paul's death?"

"She loved him very much. Who knows?"

"Surely, you don't blame yourself?"

"No," he replied, with a shake of the head. "No. Yes, of course I do."

Eleanor looked at him, resisted the temptation to melt into his arms. She sensed there was more. More confessions.

"So, what was it you fell out over?"

"A woman," he admitted, guiltily. "Helen Fulshawe!" Adam blurted out the next moment.

Eleanor suddenly remembered the references in Dave's letters to the Wingco's 'mystery woman', with whom Adam had once been besotted, remembered also Adam's drunken lament that he had killed Bert Fulshawe.

"Wing-Commander Fulshawe's wife?" She inquired, stupidly.

"I think Bert found out about it just before he killed himself."

Eleanor stared at the man.

"He killed himself..."

"The story about a crash was Group's idea."

"Oh."

"It must have all got a bit too much for him. Bert shot himself."

"Oh, dear. The poor man."

Eleanor got to her feet, crossed her arms. Guiltily she realised she did not care what had happened to Adam's predecessor. Or the reasons why. The tragedy of it meant nothing to her. Not now. It was the past, it was gone. Only the present mattered.

Was Adam still Helen Fulshawe's lover?

Did the man she loved still carry a flame for Helen Fulshawe?

And if not why was he telling her this?

Any of it?

She fought down the terror, spoke with a forced calm.

"Tell me it's over? Tell me it's over between you and her?"

Adam jumped up.

"Of course it's over!"

Eleanor threw her arms around his neck, clung to him, nestled against him as wave after wave of relief washed over her.

"It ended over a year ago."

"Good. That's all I care about. I don't care about anything else. I know it's unforgivably selfish, but I really don't care about anything that happened before we met. I don't care a fig. Not one fig!"

Adam held her tight, basked in her soft warmth and the musky scent of her hair. He planted a kiss on the top of her head, sighed.

"I love you," he murmured in her ear.

Eleanor eased herself away, turned her face to look at him. Her eyes were moist, glistening in the gloom.

"Then marry me!" She said, recklessly.

"Will you have me?"

"If you ask me, darling."

Adam swallowed hard, took her hands in his.

"In that case. Will you, do me, the honour of marrying me?"

Eleanor giggled like a girl, lifted her mouth to his and kissed him.

Then, breathlessly.

"Of course I will, darling!"

[The End]

Author's End Note

Thank you for reading **When Winter Comes**. I hope you enjoyed it; if not, I am sorry. Either way, I still thank you for giving of your time and attention to read it. Civilisation depends on people like you.

Although all the events depicted in the narrative of **When Winter Comes** are set in a specific place and time the characters in it are the constructs of my own imagination. *Ansham Wolds, Waltham Grange, Kelmington* and *Faldwell* are fictional Bomber Command bases, likewise, *380, 388* and *647 Squadrons* exist only in my head. While *Bawtry Hall* was the Headquarters of No 1 Group, I have made no attempt to accurately depict it, or any members of the command staff posted to it in 1943 and 1944. Moreover, the words and actions attributed to specific officers at Bawtry Hall and elsewhere are *my* words.

One final thought.

A note on jargon. I have been at pains to make **When Winter Comes** accessible to readers who are relatively new to the subject matter and therefore not necessarily wholly conversant with the technologies and contemporary Royal Air Force 'service speak'; while attempting *not* to sacrifice the atmosphere and *reality* of that subject matter for readers who are already immersed in Bomber Command's campaigns. For example, I describe aircraft by employing their designated 'letters' – that is, B-Baker, or T-Tommy and so on – rather than using the common RAF parlance of referring to an aircraft by its serial number. Likewise, where possible I look to explain technical terms and procedures in layperson's language. Inevitably, this leaves one open to the charge that one is 'dumbing down'; but there are many trade-offs in writing any serious work of fiction, and I sincerely hope I have drawn the line in more or less the right place. However, this is a judgement I leave to you, my reader.

Other Books by James Philip

The Timeline 10/27/62 World

The Timeline 10/27/62 - Main Series

Book 1: Operation Anadyr
Book 2: Love is Strange
Book 3: The Pillars of Hercules
Book 4: Red Dawn
Book 5: The Burning Time
Book 6: Tales of Brave Ulysses
Book 7: A Line in the Sand
Book 8: The Mountains of the Moon
Book 9: All Along the Watchtower
Book 10: Crow on the Cradle
Book 11: 1966 & All That

A standalone Timeline 10/27/62 Novel

Football In The Ruins – The World Cup of 1966

Coming in 2018-19

Book 12: Only In America
Book 13: Warsaw Concerto

Timeline 10/27/62 - USA

Book 1: Aftermath
Book 2: California Dreaming
Book 3: The Great Society
Book 4: Ask Not of Your Country
Book 5: The American Dream

Timeline 10/27/62 – Australia

Book 1: Cricket on the Beach
Book 2: Operation Manna

Other Series & Books

The Guy Winter Mysteries

Prologue: Winter's Pearl
Book 1: Winter's War
Book 2: Winter's Revenge
Book 3: Winter's Exile
Book 4: Winter's Return
Book 5: Winter's Spy
Book 6: Winter's Nemesis

The Harry Waters Series

Book 1: Islands of No Return
Book 2: Heroes
Book 3: Brothers in Arms

The Frankie Ransom Series

Book 1: A Ransom for Two Roses
Book 2: The Plains of Waterloo
Book 3: The Nantucket Sleighride

The Strangers Bureau Series

Book 1: Interlopers
Book 2: Pictures of Lily

NON-FICTION CRICKET BOOKS

FS Jackson
Lord Hawke

Audio Books of the following Titles are available (or are in production) now

Aftermath
After Midnight
A Ransom for Two Roses
Brothers in Arms
California Dreaming
Heroes
Islands of No Return
Love is Strange
Main Force Country
Operation Anadyr
The Big City
The Cloud Walkers
The Nantucket Sleighride
The Painter
The Pillars of Hercules
The Road to Berlin
The Plains of Waterloo
Until the Night
When Winter Comes
Winter's Exile
Winter's Nemesis
Winter's Pearl
Winter's Return
Winter's Revenge
Winter's Spy
Winter's War

Cricket Books edited by James Philip

The James D. Coldham Series
[Edited by James Philip]

Books

Northamptonshire Cricket: A History [1741-1958]
Lord Harris

Anthologies

Volume 1: Notes & Articles
Volume 2: Monographs No. 1 to 8

Monographs

No. 1 - William Brockwell
No. 2 - German Cricket
No. 3 - Devon Cricket
No. 4 - R.S. Holmes
No. 5 - Collectors & Collecting
No. 6 - Early Cricket Reporters
No. 7 – Northamptonshire
No. 8 - Cricket & Authors

———

Details of all James Philip's books and forthcoming publications
will be found on his website www.jamesphilip.co.uk

Cover artwork concepts by James Philip
Graphic Design by Beastleigh Web Design

Printed in Poland
by Amazon Fulfillment
Poland Sp. z o.o., Wrocław